SAVING
EL CHICO

SAVING EL CHICO

META F. STRAUSS

To Jan —
thinking of 2016 —
bringing in home —
at your home! in style!
Looking for more
good times! Happy trails!
Meta

ECOM Publishing
Sonoma, California 95476

Editing by Deb Carlen

Cover by Fena

ISBN – 13:978-1502479389
ISBN – 10:1502479389

For

David, Elizabeth, Christine, Jon, Bart, Erica,
Emma, Colton, Ozro, Manda
and all Texans wherever you reside

TABLE OF CONTENTS

1	Water	24	Progress
2	Silver Crow	25	Fire
3	Percy and Graystone	26	Teamwork
4	Annie's Tea Room	27	Billy and Dolly
5	The Mountain	28	Cars
6	Cut 'n Curl	29	Founders Day Parade
7	Jake	30	The Festival
8	Jake and Silver Crow	31	Advice
9	Jake and Bea	32	More Crime
10	Bea	33	Taxes or Prayer
11	The Ladies	34	Real Estate
12	Ed	35	Bea and Nick
13	Farnsworth's	36	Council Meeting
14	City Council	37	New Preacher
15	Church	38	Discovery
16	Music	39	The Plan
17	Sweet Charity	40	Dude Visits the Ranch
18	Cats and Cactus	41	The Ceremony
19	Percy	42	Enigma
20	Old Friends	43	Miracles
21	The Tower	44	Wee Small Hours
22	Be Lovely Boutique	45	Blueprint
23	The Men	46	On the Road Again

MAP OF EL CHICO

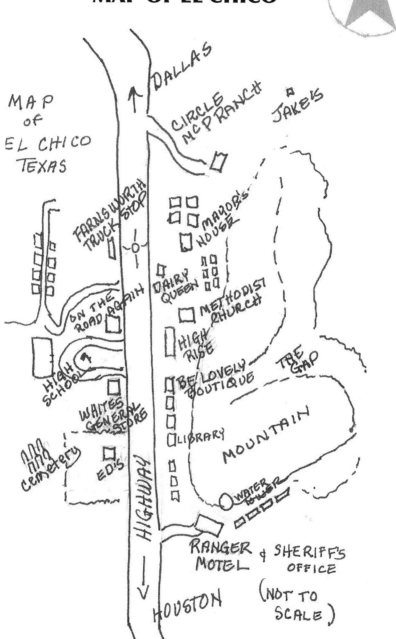

MAP
of
EL CHICO
TEXAS

DALLAS

CIRCLE McP RANCH

JAKE'S

FARNSWORTH TRUCK STOP

MAYOR'S HOUSE

DAIRY QUEEN

METHODIST CHURCH

ON THE ROAD AGAIN

HIGH RISE

BE LOVELY BOUTIQUE

THE GAP

HIGH SCHOOL

WHITES GENERAL STORE

LIBRARY

MOUNTAIN

cemetery

ED'S

WATER TOWER

HIGHWAY

RANGER MOTEL & SHERIFF'S OFFICE

(NOT TO SCALE)

HOUSTON

ix

CHARACTERS

Jake Johnson	Cowboy Foreman of Circle McP Ranch
Bea McPherson	Owner of Circle McP Ranch
Harold McPherson	Bea's brother
Silver Crow Parker	Great Grandson of Quanah Parker
Percy Foremost	Mayor
Etta Ruth Foremost	Mayor's wife
Nicholas Graystone	CEO of H_2O Engineering Firm
Ed Hawkins	Owner Ed's Salvage Yard & Golf Course, City Council Member
Odelia Marie Hawkins	Ed's wife
Chester Cartwright	Handyman
Violet Cartwright	Chester's wife, Town Librarian
Minnie Lee Gibbons	Member of Church Lady's Guild
B.J. "Bubba" Neighbors	High School Coach
Ethel Ogletree	President of Senior Residence
Doug Farnsworth	Owner of Farnsworth Truck Stop, City Council Member
Wanda Farnsworth	Doug's wife
Joe Farnsworth	Farnsworth's son, Musician
Juan Martinez	Trucker
Big Al Mosley	Trucker
Dalton Darnell	Sheriff
Henry Logan	Town Drunk
Oliver Brumfeld	Town Bachelor, City Council Member

Lester Plunker	El Chico Bank President, City Council Member
Marjorie Plunker	President of Church Lady's Guild, Lester's wife
Wilmur White	Owner of General Store, City Council Member
Gaylene White	Wilmur's wife
Clarajean White	Wilmur's daughter, Singer
Herb Matson	Accountant, City Council Member
Mary Nelle Matson	Herb's wife
Buzzie Adams	Owner of Ranger Motel, Deputy Sheriff
Annie Adams	Buzzie's wife
Isaiah Paul Pevey	Methodist Minister
Myrtle Pevey	Wife of Reverend Pevey
Geraldine Whitfield	Myrtle's friend
Billy Nelson	Owner of On the Road Again Bar & Grill
Dolly Nelson	Billy's wife
Lulu Belle Schwartz	Owner of Be Lovely Boutique & Cut 'n Curl Salon
Juanita Gutierrez	Dairy Queen Manager
Jose' Gutierrez	Juanita's husband
James Hanson	New Methodist Minister
Adelle Smith Hanson	James's wife
Jim Junior & Baines	Son's of James and Adelle
Gavin Atherson	Geologist

PROLOGUE

Rocks tumbled down the mountainside as horse and rider made their way down a dry creek bed. Jake Johnson squinted, pulling down his large, sweat-stained Stetson to avoid the blinding sunlight. A crowd of buzzards circled, then feasted on small animals dead from dehydration. There was not a cloud in the sky or a sign of water anywhere on the ranch. The cowboy thought of past times when massive cattle herds grazed here in deep grass. He sighed, turned his horse and galloped across the barren, mesquite-dotted prairie, leaving a trail of dust.

WATER

Rotund Mayor Percy Foremost, the sleeves of his plaid western shirt rolled up to the elbows, thumped the microphone; its loud whistle quieted the group. He fingered his handlebar mustache to make sure it still curled upward and hadn't wilted in the heat.

"First of all, I want to thank y'all for coming out tonight. You know why we're here. When we turn on our faucets all we get is a slow stream of mostly rusty water 'cause our city well is at a critical low point. We know the aquifer is dryin up. Cattle are dying on our ranches and cotton crops are a thing of the past. Y'all want to know how El Chico can survive, or if El Chico can survive in the twenty-first century. The town needs community action, and fast, which is why I called this emergency town meetin."

The sweltering El Chico High School gym was packed. Eager citizens were pressed body-to-body into hard bleacher seats. On the opposite side of the facility, a row of large fans went full blast, circulating hot air. Two elderly ladies were escorted outside, friends fearful they'd have heart attacks.

Junior Neighbors, captain of the Horn Toad Football team, lead the Pledge of Allegiance. Brother Pevey, the Methodist Minister, delivered the invocation and Clarajean White sang her rendition of "God Bless America." When the traditional opening ceremony to all El Chico gatherings ended, the mayor regained the microphone, prompting the restless crowd to chant, "We want water! We want rain!"

The mayor's arms went up. "Quiet. Quiet." The crowd obeyed. "This evening I have the privilege of introducing an expert in the field of water conservation. I met this fine man at the West Texas

Mayors' Conference last year and invited him to speak at this special gathering. He has come all the way from Dallas to share up-to-date drought information with us, right here, right now, tonight. His engineering degree is from Texas A&M." The introduction was interrupted by a zealous, "Gig 'em, Aggies!" The guest speaker raised his fist, extending his thumb in the school's familiar sign. A few A&M supporters cheered, reviving the sluggish throng.

"As I was sayin, let's welcome a former member of the Texas Drought Preparedness Council **and** a former member of the Dallas Cowboy football team." Motioning to the movie-star handsome man, the mayor raised his voice. "Here is my friend, Mr. Nicholas Graystone." The crowd stood and cheered. It was a first to have a real Dallas Cowboy visit El Chico.

Graystone laid his Stetson and hand-tooled briefcase on his chair and removed his tailored western suit jacket. All six-feet-six, two-hundred-fifty pounds swaggered up to the podium. The man hoped the El Chico crowd would see the Dallas Cowboy logo crafted into the toes of his custom made red, white, and blue Nocona boots. If asked, he readily pulled up his pants leg to show the Texas flag and large lone star featured on the boot tops.

With a wide smile, revealing his perfectly aligned, bright white teeth, Nicholas Graystone brushed his hands through his sweat-drenched, dark brown hair and began his presentation.

"Ladies and gentlemen of El Chico, thank you and your mayor for allowing me to visit your fine town." The man cleared his throat. "As a member of The Texas Drought Preparedness Council, I was charged with supporting drought management efforts in the state and with conducting drought monitoring, assessment, preparedness, mitigation, and assistance."

Pointing to a display behind him, he continued. "Please notice these maps indicating topography, reservoir locations, and stream flow for the surrounding trans-Pecos area. As Mayor Foremost said before, El Chico's water supply is very low. Unless you take major action now, you'll be completely dry and unable to survive."

The crowd was silent in an effort to absorb the information. Graystone spoke for fifteen long minutes, reciting statistics and hypnotizing the lethargic, sweating citizens into a stupor.

"And I'll end letting you know H_2O Engineering is in a unique position to help you solve El Chico's water situation. Once we conduct a feasibility study for your fair city, we'll be able to present a formal plan to your council. I trust that will be approved within the next month. Thank you for havin me speak this evening."

The audience managed tepid applause and the mayor returned to the podium. "Thank you, Nick, for sharing your vast knowledge of the drought problem and offering the services of your excellent company, H_2O Engineering. Our city council looks forward to your proposal."

Shaking the mayor's hand, Nicholas Graystone leaned in and whispered in his ear. "That's the first step in our plan, Percy."

Returning his attention to the audience, the mayor continued. "None of us likes to think of our beloved El Chico dying, but that's what we're dealin with. Survival! The mic is open to any of you who have suggestions for conserving what's left of El Chico's water."

One by one the spirited El Chicans stepped to the podium and shared their ideas as council secretary and reporter for the *El Chico Times Gazette,* Bea McPherson, recorded them on a large blackboard.

1. *No outdoor watering of any kind other than for produce.*

2. *Toilet flushing limited as possible.*

3. *Sponge bathing on Mondays, Wednesdays, and Fridays; showers for 2 minutes on Tuesdays, Thursdays, Saturdays, and Sundays.*

4. *Air conditioning set at 82° or higher.*

5. *No cooking in ovens; grilling encouraged.*

SILVER CROW

The crowd became quiet. As if from thin air, a figure appeared walking the length of the school's gym towards the podium. The man gave the impression he was gliding on some kind of mystical surface. He was a striking image: dark skin stretched around high cheek bones, long braids as black as midnight streamed down his back and his eyes were as blue and clear as crystal. His boots were snakeskin, and jeans clung tight around his muscular legs. A tooled leather belt with a large silver buckle inlaid with turquoise sat low on his hips. His white, western-styled shirt was topped off with a bolo and medallion clasp. As he reached the front of the room, he raised his hands and closed his eyes. The crowd was hypnotized.

After a nervous pause, Mayor Foremost stepped forward, microphone in shaking hands. "It seems we have another speaker. Chief Parker, please introduce yourself in case there are some here who don't know you."

With the grace of a gazelle, the Native American took the mic and stepped in front of the podium. The man's voice floated over the audience. "My name is Silver Crow Parker. My great grandfather was Quanah Parker. I am Chief of the Empire of the Summer Moon. You know us as the Comanche nation. I am also Chairman of Indian Affairs for the State of Texas and am well aware of the crisis at hand. This misuse of resources has come to a point where all of us must make great sacrifices or lose what little water is left. I am sad at heart when I see our land dying." El Chico's citizens were spellbound.

The man's voice was deep and forceful, rolling across the gathering like the rumble just before a large clap of thunder. "Only because I was asked by Jake Johnson, a man who values the earth, am I here to offer my assistance." He motioned to a ruggedly good-looking man leaning against a corner wall wearing starched jeans and worn boots, holding a sweat-stained Stetson in his hands.

"I don't wish to intrude on any other part of your civic decisions, and only when asked, with the approval of your community will I and the Native American Council offer our ancient rain ceremony.

"Before the white man came, when waters dried up, The People moved from place to place giving the land time to rebuild. Now civilization has new technology able to drill deep into the earth's reserves making it possible for mankind to stay in one place for generations. That is, until the earth has no more to give. That is where El Chico is now. The great El Chico Mountain's bounty of minerals and its springs have been used up and the ground is barren. Only the Great Spirit can bring the rain and replenish the aquifer you need to sustain this town."

Silver Crow's piercing eyes gazed at the crowd. "If you, each of you, agree to respect this area's natural resources in the future, The People will conduct a sacred ceremony to bring water back to El Chico." Pausing, he added, "Let your mayor know your decision."

With that, he disappeared just as he had arrived: in an instant, like a ghost.

The mayor regained the microphone. "Thank you, Silver Crow and fellow citizens for your suggestions." Raising his voice like an evangelist at the end of a sermon he added, "and, a very special thank you to Nicholas Graystone. I'm sure our community will respond favorably to your pipeline proposal."

The crowd was leaving the gym before the mayor finished speaking, glad to end the long, hot session.

Bea McPherson, placed her reporter's notepad on her chair and gathered Graystone's charts and graphs. She didn't sense his ogling eyes as she bent over to retrieve papers that had fallen to the floor. Before he could introduce himself to the gorgeous redhead, a small crowd surrounded the ex-football player waiting to shake his hand.

Bea followed the group out the double doors to the parking lot.

She waved the dropped items in the air and yelled but Graystone was too distracted to hear her. She turned around and muttered to herself. "I'll return these when you present your proposal to the city council next month."

PERCY AND GRAYSTONE

After the gym cleared, the mayor sat alone on the empty bleachers and thought back to his introduction to Graystone. Although it had only been a year before, it seemed a lifetime.

Their friendship began at the Mayor's convention in Dallas. Percy had been anxious to hobnob with high-profile attendees. He wanted to stand out, be recognized as important. Going from meeting to meeting, he shook hands and talked with other mayors. Percy couldn't help but compare himself to them. He felt he made a positive impression with his handlebar mustache, western style clothes, big personality, and knowledge of issues.

Much of his time was spent addressing the drought in West Texas, the main situation he was dealing with in El Chico and the reason the city paid for the trip. He listened to one speech after another by experts on the subject. Nicholas Graystone was on a panel at an early morning seminar discussing the idea of engineered water systems for drought-stricken communities. Percy was impressed by the man's striking appearance and apparent knowledge of pipelines and aquifer levels. As always, Percy stood and asked questions at the end of the session using as many big words as he could. He reasoned that was one way to be noticed and remembered as a significant member of the conference.

Later, Percy sat by himself at the Dallas Ritz-Carlton bar assessing the day. He sipped a Mojito, something people in El Chico had never tasted and he'd never heard of until this trip. He wondered why he had settled for small town life as he looked around at the elaborate room with its contemporary furnishings and fancy recessed lighting. Soft jazz filtered through hidden speakers and crystal glasses clinked as bartenders served the sophisticated crowd. The place even smelled like success with traces of perfume and bourbon permeating the air. It was nothing like El Chico, and Percy liked it.

When he was a pre-law student he worked his way through Sam Houston State University in Huntsville as a maintenance attendant at the nearby prison. As he mopped floors Percy dreamed of being rich and maybe becoming a celebrity. He wanted to be far away from his poor roots and the grandparents who raised him after his drunken parents did a death dive in their family station wagon off a Brazos River bridge.

At a friend's fraternity party, his buddy pointed out Etta Ruth Watson, explaining she came from a very wealthy west Texas family. She was cute, perky and sexy. Percy pursued her and by the end of the semester won her heart. At the time he thought her family's wealth and status would satisfy his ambitions. But, here he was twenty-four years later: a chubby middle-aged man who never passed the bar exam. His biggest achievement was becoming the mayor of a tiny metropolis. He was dissatisfied, disappointed and frustrated. Percy wanted more. He wanted to be like some of the people in that very room.

"Hey there! Aren't you the Houston mayor?" A stunning, sexy blond sat beside him at the bar.

Percy was startled and turned to see if the woman was really talking to him. When he saw she was, he smiled. "Well, not the Houston mayor, but I am a mayor."

"Oh, I knew you were someone important. You just have that look." She nodded to the bartender and he brought her and the mayor matching martinis.

"Yes mam, I'm from a thriving town in west Texas, El Chico. We're a small but very progressive ranching community. Maybe you've heard of us?"

"Hmmm. El Chico. It's out there close to Abilene, right?"

"So, you do know El Chico?"

The woman nodded, recognizing that any little west Texas town could be described as near Abilene. "Tell me Mr. Mayor, how did you get in the mayoring business?"

That's all it took for Percy to launch the embellished version of his life, the same tale he divulged to anyone at the convention who would listen. He described his real estate business, his big home, the long history of the family's glass factory and then the discovery of oil, never mentioning it was all his wife's fortune, not his. After another martini Percy was laughing and joking with everyone at the bar. The woman, Janelle, suggested they sit at a nearby booth where they could have a more intimate visit.

As they walked to the table, the very tall, handsome man from the morning's engineering panel approached them. Percy watched as Janelle and the man exchanged friendly kisses. "Percy, this is my longtime friend and boss, Nick Graystone, owner of H2O Engineering. I know you remember seeing him play football for the Cowboys. And, Nick, this is Percy Foremost, the honorable mayor of El Chico. You've surely heard about him and his involvement solving the drought situation. He has the kind of background the state looks for over in Austin."

"It's a pleasure to meet you." The tall man bent over and shook the mayor's hand like it was the biggest honor he'd ever encountered. "You were in the meeting this morning and asked some very insightful questions. I heard about your good work over in West Texas and understand some of the challenges."

Nick didn't move, forcing Percy to ask him to join them. The threesome talked and drank. Percy consumed more alcohol than he could remember drinking at one time. Sitting with a real Dallas Cowboy and a sophisticated woman was a dream. Percy's loose lips continued to spout information about how he was elected for three terms, in landslides, and about his power and prestige around the El Chico area.

Nick explained how his engineering firm specialized in water remediation as well as real estate ventures throughout the state. "It seems the two of us have a lot in common. We'll have to get together sometime and see if we can do some business."

Under the table, as the men talked about the drought, Janelle stroked Percy's thigh. His body was in full response mode something it hadn't been in years. He could hardly breathe and prayed Graystone didn't notice.

The next morning Percy awoke in his hotel room with a huge hangover and memories of Janelle kissing him good-bye, handing him her H2O business card and saying she hoped they'd meet again. As he savored the evening's memories and the sensation of Janelle, his phone rang.

It was Graystone. "Hey there, Mr. Mayor."

Percy listened to Nick's invitation. "Sure, it'll be good for us to get together and discuss my town's drought situation. I'm not sure how H2O can help us, but talking never hurts. Yes, in two weeks I can be back in Dallas." All Percy really thought about was the possibility of getting to see Nick's assistant once more.

That was how Percy's involvement with Graystone and Janelle started.

☆ ☆ ☆

A day after the bar encounter, unknown to Percy, Graystone talked to Janelle on his cell phone as he drove to play golf. "Yeah. I told you, I think Percy fits what I'm looking for. He put some kind of real estate deal together a couple of years ago. There's lots of personal money there and I researched the town's treasury. It's full of unallocated cash. The place is fading fast, but until the '70s it was quite the success story. Can you believe this, El Chico doesn't even run on computers?"

"Well, honey, sounds like you're onto something and just in time. I made sure we have use of the office space on the dates you requested. Everything will be set up for you."

"Great. I'll arrange for Percy's visit when it's ours. Be sure to get that logo put on the front door."

"You know I'll take care of it, Nick. Do remember you're sliding by on the Lexus lease payments and your bank account is looking like this drought you keep talking about."

"You don't have to remind me, Janelle." Graystone grimaced. "Things will fall into place. They always have."

Janelle applied her make-up as she talked to Graystone from her home. "That Percy was a piece of work. He's kinda cute but definitely not my style. 'Way too West Texas for me."

"I think you gave ole Percy the time of his life." Graystone snickered. "So, you'll get those photos framed and hung like we discussed?"

"Absolutely. The office will showcase all the projects and awards you never had." She chortled. "Nick, I was glad to help you out last night. Who knew? Maybe I would've liked him. Find me another guy, okay? Preferably single. And this time a big city mayor, or introduce me to one of your rich retired football-player-friends."

While Janelle chitchatted in his ear, Nick's thoughts flashed back to his youth. He grew up living in a small garage apartment at the back of a sprawling Houston estate. This, and tuition to a fashionable private school, was provided as part of the compensation given to his widowed mother who was the personal assistant to a wealthy oil man's high society wife. Nick winced as he remembered being teased by his rich classmates as the school's misfit: a short, fat kid that didn't have money and came from the wrong side of society. A smile crossed his face when he thought about his quick growth spurt in the 9th grade and how he had morphed into a very tall, slender and nice looking teen. He used these attributes to become a popular star athlete. When he received a full scholarship to Texas A&M he vowed to his mother he'd become rich and powerful one day. No matter what he had to do, she would never have to work again. His mom died when he was a junior in college, never able to see her son achieve his goals.

Two weeks after the Mayor's Conference, Percy made a trip to Dallas at Nick's request.

Nick, wearing his trademark western styled suit (this time beige with dark brown trim and matching alligator boots), waved to the man standing in the hotel lobby nervously twisting his mustache. "My car is parked right outside." He shook Percy's hand, patted his back and winked. "I hope you've been giving some thought to how we might make something big happen over in El Chico."

The mayor talked as Graystone drove down Stemmons Freeway. "I've been thinkin, Nick. El Chico is hurtin from lack of water and I'd like to hear more about your water pipeline experiences."

Graystone turned into a circular drive landscaped with rows of manicured hedges. He parked in a reserved parking spot and led the small town mayor into the foyer of the contemporary glass and metal skyscraper that housed H2O Engineering. Percy's eyes grew large with wonder and admiration.

"Well, Percy, our firm has worked on many projects for small water districts like yours." Graystone pressed the elevator button and the two exited on the fifteenth floor. "Here we are in my little kingdom." Graystone smiled as he opened the beveled glass door into a large reception room lined with leather chairs. Western oil paintings hung on the walls.

There, at the large wraparound reception desk, was Janelle. Percy nearly fainted. She was more beautiful than he remembered.

"Hi there, Mr. Mayor." Janelle walked to Percy and gave him a hug. "Welcome to H2O."

"Percy, I guess we told you that Janelle's been my right-hand man for years."

"Uh. No. Yes. Y'all did mention that." Percy's heart rate went up. He hoped the pair didn't notice he was sweating at the sight of the curvaceous blond. "It's good to see you again," was the only greeting Percy could manage to force from his mouth.

Janelle smiled and returned to the desk. "I'll see you two later. If you need anything, just holler."

"Follow me." Graystone continued talking as he showed El Chico's mayor one unmanned office after another. "The rest of my staff is all out in the field, as you can see." Graystone poured drinks for himself and the mayor from his office bar. "Here's to friendship, Percy." The men clinked glasses.

The mayor was euphoric as he gazed at the Dallas skyline and walked around the massive corner office. "Nick, is this you in the photo with President Bush?"

"Oh, yeah. There's several with both Presidents Bush and with the Clintons. You might be interested in these photos." He pointed out several framed pictures. "They're some of our more successful projects."

"Very impressive, Nick." Percy sipped on his drink as he walked around looking at photos of pipelines, towers, and Nick with celebrities and football players. He had no idea most were fabricated and were no more real than Elvis on velvet.

Nick pointed to a series of photos. "Percy, this project was so successful these clients not only saved their town, but were able to put in an "A" Class resort. They're raking in millions. Of course, you probably don't have that kind of property over in El Chico or the investment funds. It takes lots of influence to put something like that together."

Percy looked carefully at the images of the elaborate resort and, just as Graystone hoped, thought how great a place like that would look with El Chico's mountain in the background.

"You like steak, Percy?"

"Hell, yes. I'm a Texan."

"Then I want to take you to one of my favorite restaurants."

As the two men passed Janelle, Graystone said, "Janelle, why don't you join us for dinner? You don't mind, do you, Percy?" The El Chico mayor felt the day was looking like one of the best in his life.

✯ ✯ ✯

Over the next months Percy and Nick discussed the idea of a pipeline and reservoir solution to El Chico's water needs. Sometimes they talked on the phone and other times Percy drove to the H_2O

office then enjoyed an evening out with Graystone. Usually Janelle would join them, continuing to thrill the small town man with her attention.

Once, Nick met Percy at the hotel and drove him to his palatial home in north Dallas. Percy was awestruck when Nick manuvered up a long drive and was greeted by a maid and butler in uniforms, just like in the movies. After a gourmet meal, they gazed at Nick's pool and manicured yard while they sipped wine from Nick's cellar. Percy concluded the man must be very successful to have so much wealth just as his new friend had planned.

He didn't know the office was a shared space rented month to month with several other individuals needing an impressive façade or that the home was leased, complete with furnishings. He didn't know Nick needed to make a deal fast or he'd be living in his leased car.

"I like the idea of the pipeline, but how do I know H_2O is the right company for such a big job?" Percy felt compelled to question Nick.

"First of all, I would never go after a project I didn't think H_2O could handle. You saw the photos in my office. That alone should confirm you can trust I know what I'm doing, have done the same thing before. If that's not enough, just look at our web site." Nick was glad Janelle had insisted on having a site.

Percy smiled and nodded his head. He didn't want Nick to know he, and half of El Chico, didn't own computers.

Nick continued, "In this extreme heat and dryness more water evaporates from the above ground lake-styled reservoirs than gets used. Basically, it's wasted. Some experts say over half goes right up into the sky. I suggest we copy what's going on over in Nevada."

Percy listened with great interest. "What's happening there?"

Nick continued, "ASR. That's what's happening."

"What's ASR?" Acronyms impressed Percy.

"Oh. That's Aquifer Storage and Recovery systems. Folks in the water-getting business say it's an answer to the water shortage all over the country. I believe El Chico is right for it. We'll pump surface water from either the Edwards or Carrizo Reservoirs to El Chico, then inject it into your empty aquifer to store it and then pump it back up to use. That's one of the possibilities I'm suggesting for us. "

"That sounds great to me, Nick, but how do you know you can get the rights-of-way needed?"

"Well, my friend, that would be what El Chico would pay me for. By the way, I can't spend more time on this project without a retainer. I'm sure you understand that. And, Mr. Mayor, it will be your job to get those funds from your fair city and allocate them to H$_2$O."

Each meeting caused Percy to speculate about ways he could benefit from the rebirth of El Chico. Just being mayor and living in Etta's family home wasn't enough now that he'd experienced Nick's big office, his upscale home, and Janelle's presence.

His mind kept flashing pictures of the resort featured in Nick's office. Why didn't Nick think El Chico was suited for such a fine place? The mountain would be a perfect backdrop. If El Chico had water, the project would be possible. The town had a very interesting history, what with it being the former home of the Texas Rangers and land of the last free Comanche. He thought they could have a small museum showing Ranger memorabilia and Native American artifacts. Personally he didn't care for redskins, but tourists loved all that Indian stuff.

That night after the town meeting Percy sat on the gym bleachers thinking of the blond woman and how he looked forward to seeing her each time he visited Nick's Dallas office. At home he had dreamed about her. At work he thought about her walking around El Chico on his arm and about her in his bed. He knew it was wrong. He still loved Etta Ruth, but he couldn't help himself. Maybe he was finally getting the break he needed and he'd become one of Texas's elite. Maybe he could become a state senator, or maybe even governor.

Percy felt great pride when he remembered the night he made his proposal to Graystone, the one about developing a resort in El Chico. He had convinced Nick that together they could build an even finer resort than the one in the office photo. At first Nick wasn't sure, but by the end of that evening Percy had persuaded the big man to hop on board with his idea. Of course, Nick explained all his funds were tied up in other projects, but if Percy could back it, he would partner with him. Now all Percy had to do was to convince Etta Ruth to let him manage her estate the way he wanted to and, a bit more challenging, convince the El Chico Council to hire H$_2$O to build the water pipeline.

ANNIE'S TEA ROOM

Two weeks before the town meeting, Nicholas Graystone sat alone sipping weak coffee and munching a chocolate cookie. His eyes wandered around the frilly room. The peach walls were covered with rows of hanging china plates and other knick-knacks. He gazed at a flowered tablecloth covering one of the antique tables and asked himself, "Why in the hell am I meeting in this godforsaken place? The closest Starbucks must be more than a hundred miles away."

He twisted the Super Bowl ring on his left hand. Few knew that it was purchased at an auction, that the man had never been in a Super Bowl game. In fact, Nick Graystone had only warmed the Dallas Cowboy bench for two short years because he was too lazy to drag his playboy butt out of bed on time for practice. This did not deter his love of the sport or use of football connections to fund his various business schemes and lavish lifestyle.

He fumbled through a stack of papers reviewing his talking points. His fundraising plan required getting all the mayor's land and savings committed and then convincing drought-stricken El Chico citizens a water pipeline was essential or they'd die like so many other little west Texas towns. Graystone chuckled to himself. He'd known the mayor was in his hands a few months ago when Percy suggested building a resort in El Chico.

Nick smiled like a fox. *Yes sir re-bob! The ol' fish took the bait just like I thought he would. Before long I'll own him, this little community in the heart of Texas, and all the cash in their city's treasury.*

"Would you care for a refill?" A gray-haired lady wearing a checkered apron smiled. She carried a ceramic teapot brimming with the tiny restaurant's trademark Maryland Club coffee.

Graystone pointed to his now-empty china cup and saucer, watching as she refilled it with the lukewarm liquid. He sipped and almost gagged at the bland taste.

Twenty minutes and six cookies later, Percy Foremost and his wife, Etta Ruth, entered the door jingling the string of bells on the knob. The couple scanned the room and cautiously made their way to the table joining the Dallas engineer. Etta's dyed black hair was stacked high on her head with rhinestone clips holding it in place. She wore a long, lime-colored skirt and matching blouse embroidered with silver threads in a floral pattern. Her sandals matched. Sparkling chandelier earrings swayed, framing her moon shaped face and her arms were loaded with bracelets; enough to make Graystone wonder how she lifted them. He was sure her mascaraed eyelashes were false and thought they made her green eyes look like exotic bugs.

He stood and pulled a chair out for Etta. She grinned up at the former football player in admiration of the celebrity. He smiled his most engaging smile.

"It is such a pleasure to meet you at last, Etta Ruth. Percy has talked about you so much I feel like I already know you. And, Percy, glad you could meet me today." Graystone shook hands and slapped the back of the portly mayor, a shoulder shorter than his towering frame. He waved to the hostess and waited for his guests to be served some of the awful coffee and a plate of cookies.

Percy glanced outside. "I guess this was as good a place as any to get together. Seems private enough. I didn't see anyone from El Chico on the highway and I don't think they'd stop at Annie's Tea Room, anyway."

"That's good to know. For now, we have to keep our plan a complete secret." He looked to be sure Etta understood.

"Nick, Etta and I have no secrets from each other, just like I told you." He mentally added the word "almost" to that statement as he thought about Janelle. "I've explained all about our business plans for El Chico." He patted the woman's hand and smiled.

"That is just wonderful to know. Etta, the last time Percy and I talked he said the old water tank is leaking and there's very little water pressure. Makes the citizens upset enough to move."

"Of course they're upset. It takes forever to fill up a sink, and gettin enough water for a bubble bath is impossible." Etta Ruth ate a cookie as she talked.

Graystone nodded at the couple. "This works in our favor. The more people suffer from the lack of water, the faster they'll sell out and move away. As far as they'll know, the main aquifer is almost dried up."

"This bein the sixth year of the drought, no rain to speak of in a year, we don't have to do a thing to convince folks in El Chico that there's no water. By the way, Nick, there's another house goin on the market next week that we can buy cheap."

"Good sign." Graystone handed a stack of folders to the couple. "Since we're runnin late, let me get started." He pointed to one highlighted point after another. "You'll see lots of technical engineering data that shows the top level of the aquifer is depleted. That's what we'll show the citizens at the upcoming town meeting when we propose the pipeline.

"But, Percy and Etta, here's the good news for us." Graystone pulled another report from the stack. "We don't really need a pipeline. Look closely and you'll see this version shows if we drill deeper there's enough water to support the town and our building project. Drillin deeper is a minor expense compared to what we'll propose."

"Yep, I can see that. It's real convincing. Makes it easy to raise some big money. Of course drilling deep might work now but long term we're still gonna need rain."

"Percy … Etta, it's going to rain some time. It always does. Looking at the blueprints you'll see where the El Chico Mountain pass used to be a real oasis."

Etta batted her lashes, glad to be able to contribute to the discussion. "Why yes, Nick, it was the place cattle drives stopped for a couple of days so herds could fill up with fresh water on their way to Abilene, Kansas from South Texas."

"Etta dear, you'll be glad to know that's where we'll build the major part of our resort." The Dallas man continued to smile at Percy's wife.

Percy's expression was serious. "Uhh. I see you have drawings for the pipeline going from the Ivie Reservoir to El Chico. This will be great to show the City Council when you make your proposal." Percy frowned, smiled, grimaced, and adjusted his bifocals flipping through the data marking here and there with a red pen. "How much will we say this pipeline costs?"

Graystone smiled, "I have some figures on page 21 of the report but I'm still gathering bids. If we can convince El Chico's council to hire H_2O for the study, making a down payment right away, balance due at project completion, we can begin the first steps in our plan. With your influence I'm sure that'll happen."

The mayor's chest puffed out in pride. "I did win the past three elections in landslides."

"Once we have those funds we can start buying more property located in the resort perimeters. Those parcels you acquired when you built the senior apartment center are perfectly located. I see nothing but success for us in the future. I'm setting up a corporate identity now and of course, you'll be included as senior partners."

Percy persisted in trying to impress the Dallas man by rummaging through the pipeline schematics jotting notes here and there. "And you think I need to start buying up more property now?"

"Yes, as it comes available you'll buy in the name of the corporation. The legal work will be done in Ft. Worth so there's no association locally with your name. We need funds right now to open a bank account and file some corporate paperwork before we can make our first acquisition." The large man continued his pitch to the couple, pointing to pages of numbers that appeared to offer further evidence the couple should invest. "Your initial installment will be your commitment to our venture. If you prefer to keep your cash, you can sign over a land deed as collateral. I'd like to get this finalized right away."

Percy reached over and took his wife's hand. Her fingernails glistened with the lavender glitter polish she chose at the Cut 'n Curl the day before. "Of course, Etta darlin, it's your family money and land that will have to fund our part of the investment."

Looking at the mayor's wife, Graystone slid another folder across the table knowing it would cement the deal. "Here are some drawings of the resort." Winking at Percy he added, "It includes a major golf course. Think what it would be like to have an annual PGA tournament in El Chico."

Percy's face blushed from excitement.

Etta opened the embossed folder. "Oooo, this looks soooo fabulous. I guess this is the hotel."

"Yes. This is the architectural rendering. The main building will be located at the foot of the mountain across from where the current motel is. Notice the garden trail leading to the back pool area and up the side of the limestone embankment. I was thinking we might like to name the hotel, "The Etta."

"Oh, my God. Could we really? Oh, Percy, that would be wonderful. A hotel named for me!" Percy grinned and looked at Graystone. He waited for his wife to hear the final point that was sure to make her agree to invest her inheritance in the project.

"Why, Etta, we could even rename the town Ettaville," said Nick.

For thirty minutes the three discussed details of the resort that would replace the entire east side of El Chico. "Notice we would leave the school and housing area on the west side of town as home for future employees of the complex. Just think how many jobs there'll be with a prestigious resort like ours."

"But what about all the people who live in El Chico now?" Etta frowned.

"Don't worry your pretty head about that."

"Oh, y'all, I'll have to give this lots of thought. I'm not sure they'll ever give up their property. Most've lived here all their lives and I just cain't imagine them working at a resort."

"I've been through these kinds of transitions many times. Once it happens even the most ardent opposition ends up thrilled with a new town like the one we'll build.

"I agree, Etta. The cattle business is dyin. It's a thing of the past just like the Indians, the silica mine, and the glass factory. With this drought, the whole town is going down. The water supply is dryin up and steady rain ain't comin. That's all that might save El Chico, and that would take nothin short of a miracle. With all we've done for these people, we deserve to be a major part of the redevelopment."

Looking at the mayor, Graystone continued, "As we discussed before, Percy, the idea of a pipeline with a new water tower and pumping system has to be put before your town council. You and I know the pipeline won't be necessary once we drill deeper but we need to raise tax dollars to back the real estate venture and a pipeline project is the easiest way to do it."

"Yeah. I shared your ideas with Etta Ruth. Building a water tower with a working pump system would be a good starting point. We can get an allocation from current funds to pay H_2O and to start the tower. Once everyone sees a big tower going up, it will be easy to get a tax increase voted on and passed for the ongoing project."

"I guess y'all have it figured out." Etta giggled to her husband and smiled at the handsome man from Dallas. "Percy darlin, and Nick, I think my daddy, bless his soul, would approve of using the big house and some of our savings to get our part of the investment started. Of course, you and I'll have to talk about this some more, won't we, Percy dear?"

"You two have lots to talk about." Graystone gathered up all the folders and put them in his hand-tooled leather briefcase. "I'll see you at the big town meeting, Percy. And, Etta," he took the woman's plump hand in his and kissed it, "It's a treat to meet you, dear." He left a twenty-dollar bill on the table and tipped his hat on his way out of the tearoom.

Etta and Percy gobbled the remaining cookies as they watched the white Lexus with the maroon stripes drive away.

"The man is gonna have to start drivin American-made if he wants to impress people in El Chico," said Etta Ruth.

The couple drove home across the prairie, discussing the deal that would risk their savings and do away with the little town, as it existed, giving them a chance at the riches and prestige they craved.

THE MOUNTAIN

Four generations before, Etta Ruth's ancestors were some of the first white settlers in El Chico. As they trekked across hundreds of miles of flat prairie looking for a homeland they were drawn to one single shape sticking up like a pyramid in the desert. The large mountain was not part of a range but a result of a powerful earthquake eons ago. It was created with an abundance of easy-to-mine minerals and surrounded by natural springs.

The top third of the peak was almost pure silicon dioxide sparkling in the sunlight. From a distance it looked like a large diamond. For a thousand years before the white man made his way into West Texas, Native Americans worshiped the mountain's highest point, making it sacred ground.

The last natives were Comanche. They were run out or killed when Etta's ancestors and other Irish and German settlers formed El Chico. By the late 1800s and early 1900s El Chico had become a bustling silica-mining town. So much so that Southern Pacific extended tracks to El Chico, piling rail cars high with the shiny rocks needed to make tempered glass.

A glass plant, founded by Etta's grandfather in the 1920s, added to the prosperity. Manufacturers from as far away as New York and Los Angeles used El Chico's milk, cola, and whiskey bottles. However, by the early 60s, the silica was mined out, the glass factory closed, and El Chico lost its industrial momentum. Only five blocks of mostly vacant buildings survived.

Black gold was discovered mid century, further scarring the once magnificent peak. Ugly black oil pumps raped the mountain, sucking out the remaining minerals stored in its heart. This made Etta's family and others into overnight millionaires.

By the end of the twentieth century the landmark was chopped off and bare, leaving only a naked, rocky plateau. The sacred mesa became home to monster rattlesnakes, yet the spot remained magical, a mountain high point with a panoramic view of the southern Great Plains.

CUT 'N CURL

Daytime temperatures hit 110 degrees for sixteen days in a row, setting a new record. A breeze felt like the blast one felt when first opening a hot oven door. Drivers who planned to take the scenic route across Texas opted for the Interstate where they could go fast from one point to another, bypassing El Chico. Puzzle piece cracks in the ground were wide enough to catch lambs' feet, and they did. Some citizens were afraid coffins in the cemetery would start pushing up through the dry, blown ground.

El Chico was in a funk. Instead of playing a round at Ed's Golf Course, men gathered at the Dairy Queen, sipping big plastic cups of sweet iced tea with lemon. The only thing library books were good for was fanning. The On the Road Again Bar and Grill couldn't interest a soul in brisket, and chili had become a dirty word.

Today was Friday and Lulu Belle Schwartz put the Cut 'n Curl notice under the Be Lovely Boutique sign, reminding everybody about the additional services she offered on Fridays. As she put one of her regulars under the dryer, she announced to customers sitting in various stages of getting beautiful, "I'm telling you right now. I've never seen so many people sleeping through a sermon as on this past Sunday. Brother Peavey preached about droughts and famines repeating the same verses he has every Sunday."

"I know what you mean," said Odelia Hawkins. "The Baptists are just as bored as all you Methodists with talk about drought, drought, drought. If I have to hear John 4:14 one more time I'll scream."

"I know the situation is dire and that we all need to pray for deliverance, but give us a break!" Lulu Belle arranged her supplies for the next patron.

Ethel Ogletree wiggled in the shop's door wearing one of her ever-present hats, this time topped with what appeared to be an assortment of feathers. Her ample seventy-year-old body was perched on her signature three-inch high heels. The practice of wearing such shoes was perilous to most women in her age group, but Ethel went everywhere tip-tapping in spikes. She hung her hat on the rack and sat down. "Is this what Ed got you over in Abilene?" She pointed to the fuchsia flowered swivel chair in front of the shop's large mirror.

"Yep, he delivered it yesterday and you'll be one of the first to get to sit in it." Looking around at the shop's faded wallpaper, Lulu Belle frowned. "I'll be redecoratin unless the whole town actually dries up and dies. I saw some real pretty beauty shop accessories in a catalog yesterday."

Ethel maneuvered into the chair. "As spokesperson for the El Chico High Rise Apartments and the town's only pool, I have an important announcement. Yesterday we senior citizens voted unanimously to invite all El Chico residents, including you girls, to swim any afternoon after three when we have completed our naptime. So, put on your suits and come get cooled off."

"That's fabulous news!" Lulu giggled. "And, I just happen to have a new shipment of swimwear in your sizes."

The chitchat continued about the heat and the drought. The group knew that without water they were in for worse times. El Chico was not a Mecca of commerce in a *good* year. Without water their community's lifeblood cattle business would be completely gone.

JAKE

Down the street, Jake Johnson sauntered across the ancient wood floors of Whites General Mercantile and Grocery Store, boots and floor creaking, a cadence and particular sound that was familiar in the few remaining ranch towns across Texas. "Mornin Clarajean. Came to get my usual."

She smiled, raking her fingers through her long chestnut hair. "I'm singin at the On the Road Again Saturday night." The young woman reached under the counter and handed a pint bottle of Southern Comfort to the good-looking lanky man. His Wrangler jeans were faded just like the blue denim shirt he wore. Waves of sandy-gray hair rested on his collar. The toes of his ostrich skin boots were turned up with wear.

Jake paid with cash, his mouth curling into a smile that set deep dimples into his square jaw. "Glad you're singin regular. You got real talent, young lady."

Clarajean watched the cowboy's bowlegged stride as he turned around and walked out. The warped screen door was still flapping when he got back into his rattletrap pickup. She heard the hollow clank of the door as it slammed shut.

Jake patted Sam, his sidekick, and the large yellow Lab licked his face. Then Jake untwisted the bottle cap and took his first long swig of the day. He sighed deeply as the warmth spread to his heart, down his arms and into his legs.

The cowboy turned the key, double-pumped the gas and maneuvered the temperamental gearshift lever into reverse. His boss and friend, Bea McPherson, offered to get him a new truck, but he had no use for some shiny thing he'd just have to get to know. He liked the faded Circle McP brand on the door, and each rusty dent represented a memory.

Jake drove through town past the Dairy Queen, the Farnsworth Truck Stop, and into the countryside. He glanced at the mountain, remembering when sparkling creeks lined with cottonwood trees crisscrossed the terrain. Now this part of Texas was home to mesquite trees, cactus, and large parcels of fallow land that used to be productive ranches. Until the drought, there had always been enough grass to raise premium cattle. Each spring, bluebonnets, Indian paintbrush, and other wildflowers colored the landscape like patriotic rainbows providing perfect surroundings for new calves and family picnics.

The truck bumped down the rocky road on the backside of the ranch. Jake stopped and opened the glove compartment to take another sip of Southern Comfort. The liquor going down his gullet soothed his soul. He swung down from the cab kicking dust as he untwisted the chain lock, opened the heavy metal gate, drove through, and locked it behind him. The McPhersons had trusted him to manage the Circle McP for most of his adult life. In turn they gave him good-enough pay and the 1890s-era cabin to live in. It suited him perfectly. He didn't need anything fancy; in fact, he preferred not to have any newfangled gadgets.

JAKE AND SILVER CROW

From the time he was six, Jake sensed he'd been born a century too late. As he watched John Wayne movies, he knew in his gut he belonged in the world of open spaces, cattle and cowboys. When his fourth grade class visited a ranch he touched his first horse and without thinking knew in his bones how to look into the large brown eyes, how to touch the animal firmly: it was heaven when he placed his nose against the soft pallet between the horse's nostrils.

When Jake was in high school 4-H, he won a summer work-study program on a working cattle ranch. This experience cemented the path he chose for the rest of his life. Each evening after dinner with the ranch hands, he rode his favorite horse to the outskirts of the property. Riding the small Paint mare bareback into the wilderness of West Texas was like going back in time.

One night he dismounted at a limestone rise on the side of the mountain overlooking a mesquite-covered lowland. Far below, a bubbling creek reflected a full moon. The prairie glowed as if floodlights were focused on a stage. It was the prettiest sight he'd ever seen. His reverie was interrupted by a swift blow to the back of his knees, landing him face down on the hard ground. When he caught his breath he found himself beneath a black-haired, dark-skinned, blue-eyed male about his age.

"What're you doing here?" The stranger kept his captive pinned to the rocky earth. "This is my land and always has been. My people owned it until your people massacred most all of us."

Without answering, Jake kicked and bolted, throwing the mystery attacker several feet into the air. Their bodies tangled and a long, all-out bloody fight followed, until both lay prone, unable to move. Then the two young men locked eyes. Some private unsaid communication passed between them and a century of history flowed from one to the other. Then they convulsed with laughter, rolling around on the ground like two young pups.

Jake explained his city upbringing to Silver Crow, how it never fit, how his gut told him he was meant to live in this precise area of the Texas outback. Silver Crow spoke of his grandfather, the great Quanah Parker, last chief of the Comanche nation, about his half-breed heritage and how he knew he always had been and always would be a part of this patch of earth. Thus began the deep friendship of Jake Johnson and Silver Crow Parker.

As the pickup made its way over the rough terrain, Jake gave his dog a pat. Sam followed Jake to the heap of weathered wood known as the southern barn where Jake's Appaloosa waited to begin the day's work. Pearce snorted when the hand-tooled leather saddle was thrown on and tightened. Jake mounted the large horse and began his rounds. Sam followed as they made their way down the fence line checking for breaks and any sign of water.

Dark billows formed in the distant sky. Jake frowned and shook his head. "Heaven knows we need some rain," the cowboy told his horse. "I hate these damned fickle no-rain clouds, 'specially their dry lightnin.'"

Stormy weather was the only thing Jake feared. The freak hailstorm and tornado of 1989 had come without warning when he was two days into the spring roundup. The herd stampeded and they lost seven head. That was bad, but when he returned to the main ranch, he found his young bride dead in tangled wreckage. He knew mobile homes weren't stable but she had insisted on living on the ranch close to him. She had deserved so much more and he had planned to give it to her.

"Whoa there, Pearce." Jake swung to the ground. He nuzzled the horse's nose and scratched Sam behind the ears. He unscrewed the pint and rested against the fence, letting the Southern Comfort roll down his throat filling him with the peace he needed whenever he thought about Sue.

"Hey," said the familiar voice.

Without turning Jake held out the pint bottle. "Hey yourself."

Silver Crow took a swig and passed it back. Appearing like a mirage from nowhere was the norm for the Native American. It was his way, and Jake never questioned his friend's comings and goings.

The horses, dog, and men continued around the fence line, checked the pond and counted the livestock. "The herd, or what's left of it, looks worse every day. They get so hot and starved for water they just stand knee deep in the mud," said Jake.

"Yeah, one of these days you're gonna need a crane to haul them out," observed the darker skinned man. Pointing to the horizon, he added, "These are only visiting clouds. They'll pass over and the drought will continue."

"We might ought'a get out of the way of the lightnin."

They took the cutoff to Jake's cabin, where he poured the remaining liquor into two jelly jars. He handed one to his friend, who had settled into one of two old overstuffed chairs in the one-room cabin. Sam curled up in a corner, eyes closed.

"Remember how we rodeoed weekends during college breaks? My parents never would've found out if that ol' bull hadn't caught me." Jake rubbed the stubble that hid the long scar running through the cleft on his chin.

A smile crossed Silver Crow's face. "Those were the days we drank way too much Lone Star, flirted with gals in tight jeans, and danced all night to Willie's music, that is, until we'd get in a bar fight. What were we thinkin? It's a wonder we didn't land in jail." Both men laughed, leaned back in their chairs and sipped.

Jake broke the silence. "All in all life's been good. We've found what's left of unspoiled land and us two have been able to play cowboy and Indian. But now I see our dream disappearin right before our eyes."

"Damn it to hell, the mass of humanity has destroyed many of Earth's gifts. I think we're reaching the point of no return. Without water, civilization will have to abandon the land all over West Texas. Then after another century or two it'll come back into balance and be reborn," said Silver Crow putting his boots on Jake's cable-spool table.

After a pause, he continued, "I was over in Austin last week with the Indian Council and some old boys with the State Water Board were there. The state's experts gave a report about the aquifer's condition. Even if folks do conserve water, we'll need a miracle to keep El Chico going."

"Yeah, if the ground would shift and all the old springs would open up we'd have our creeks again. A miracle. That's what we need," said Jake.

"By the way, they don't think much of that Graystone character who spoke at the town meeting.

"Crow, what do you think about the council payin that city slicker to study the water situation here? I cain't believe they'd vote to do it. Somethin about that man, besides the way he looked at Bea, rubbed me the wrong way. Maybe it was them fancy boots." said Jake. "It might be good to do some modern day scoutin around and see what more you can find out about him."

"Good idea, my friend. I will."

JAKE AND BEA

At sunrise Jake Johnson hauled the big fifty-gallon water tank to the back quadrant of the ranch, the old Ford pick-up groaning and tires about to bust. As the tank drained into the trough, he studied the yellow, bluish and tan layers of limestone surrounding the nearly dry pond, which were exposed for the first time he could remember. Jake pulled out a cigarette, looked it over and returned it to the pack. It was too hot to smoke.

Sam, usually running to greet the cattle, slinked slowly at Jake's side waiting for some reassurance his man knew what to do. "Never seen nothin like this," said Jake rubbing the big straw colored dog along his back. "What we need is a good old-fashioned Indian rain dance." Sam wagged his tail.

Jake drove up the long, rocky drive leading to the sprawling old stone ranch house. Its sweeping whitewashed porch and steep tin roof provided the only attractive architectural features. The house and several ancient outlying buildings, in various stages of disrepair, were framed by a stand of scrub oaks and large cottonwoods. A trickle was all that was left of the once abundant creek flowing alongside the complex.

"Hey, Bea." Knocking the dust off his boots, Jake announced his presence at her door. Sam greeted Bea's chocolate Lab, Buster, with tail wags and sniffing. Too hot to bark, both ran under the house hoping to get cool. Bea's cats gazed with disinterest as they fanned their tails in unison.

"Come on in and get a load off for a spell." Bea opened the glass-paned door wide for the lanky cowhand. Her low-pitched voice had just a hint of gravel overlaying its velvety quality.

Sitting down at the old, pine dining table in her kitchen, she added, "Here's a glass of lemonade, not that it makes a dent in the heat."

The sight of Bea's large, oval eyes and the rust colored galaxy of tiny freckles sprinkled across her upturned nose always made Jake smile. She was tall enough to reach the top shelf in her kitchen without a ladder and her body was muscular, a perfect hourglass, shaped from years of rodeo barrel-racing and hard ranch work. He thought how little she had changed since she was fourteen when he began working for her family.

Jake reached in his worn shirt pocket and pulled out his flask. He added a few drops to the icy glass, then tilted the container towards her. Bea pushed her long red curls off her neck, smiled at the man and slid her glass over to get some of the Southern Comfort. They sipped in silence.

"The cattle are losing more weight and I don't think some of the little ones are gonna make it," frowned Jake. "Ain't ever seen nothin so sad. I talked to the meat packers up near Amarillo and they'll buy what we have. We'll keep Duke Five and three cows so we can restock. It's all I can think to do."

"It's like we thought. We're gonna lose them one way or another," said Bea sadly. "Haul them on over next week. With the pond just about dried up and our spring at a trickle, there's barely water enough for the sheep and I know how you feel about sheep."

"Yep. Dumber than dumb. I'd sooner raise rattlesnakes. Thank God you only bought two lambs and didn't want to go into the sheep-raisin business."

BEA

It was three years earlier when Buster scratched at Bea McPherson's door, wagged his tail and barked, alerting her the mail arrived. The dog always got excited when he saw the small car pull up to the aluminum box mounted beside the front gate. This signaled time for their regular quarter mile walk down the dirt drive so Bea could see what the outside world had to offer in the way of advertisements and bills.

There was a notice from the Texas Tech Alumni Association announcing a fundraising event and asking for a donation, an advertisement for White's General Mercantile Store, an electric bill, and on and on. Bea set all but one item on the fence rail, ripping open a large yellow envelope with her brother's name in the upper left corner. "Oh my God, Buster, Harold sent me a wonderful gift." She was sorting through the packet when she heard the sound of Jake's noisy pickup.

Bea jumped up and down and flashed the tickets at the foreman when he turned off the highway onto their road. Long ago Bea had given up romance with Jake, reluctantly settling for friendship, realizing he was never going to get over loosing his wife. "Jake, I can't believe it. Look what Harold sent me. I'm invited to Las Vegas."

Leaning out his pick-up window, returning her smile, Jake explored the colorful brochures and tickets waving in the warm breeze. "Harold is usually tighter than the bark on a tree, so I say, 'go,' Bea. You've never seen Vegas's bright lights and shows and I know you've wanted to."

Her hair was pulled back in a ponytail and her large emerald eyes sparkled with excitement. "Thanks, Jake. I needed you to give me the okay on this."

Jake didn't understand why Bea required his input. She was the most independent woman he had ever known. When Bea's parents were killed in a car accident ten years ago, she inherited half the 932 acres. Harold had no interest in ranch life so he sold his shares to her.

Jake understood why Bea chose to spend her life on the family ranch five miles outside El Chico, forty miles from the nearest Walmart, and several hours from Lubbock. Ranching was in her blood. He knew what few locals knew: that she graduated with a bachelors degree in animal husbandry and planned to be a vet. He saw how heartbroken she was when there wasn't enough family money or loans available for her to complete the program.

Another thing Jake didn't understand was why Bea was never interested in the series of men that pursued her. He knew she had been engaged to a fellow Tech student for a semester but broke it off, no explanation given. Instead, Bea seemed content to live alone with the six cats, her dog, a few goats, the cattle, Jake, a series of ranch employees and the two damned sheep.

What Jake didn't realize was that Bea compared every man she met to him and none measured up to his honesty, courage, kindness and rugged good looks. She stayed busy with the ranch, and the city council. Bea also had the biggest satellite dish she could buy. Every night she watched the Tonight Show just to stay updated about what was going on in the real world. One of her favorite shows was *Las Vegas* and she'd wanted to visit the exciting glitzy city ever since it aired.

When Bea called Harold to accept the invitation to join him and his wife, Mary Alice, in Vegas, she asked if they would stay at the Montecito Hotel.

"Little sister, the Montecito is only make-believe and not a real place. We're regulars at the Bellagio and that's much better, trust me! I have a suite reserved for you where you can look right out your window at musical water fountains that shoot hundreds of feet into the sky."

Harold made it big in the dot-com business years ago. He and Mary Alice (who now insisted on being referred to as "Ally") lived in what Bea called a "la-tee-da" home near San Francisco and ran with other successful techies. She visited his family a couple of times but didn't feel she fit in with their sophisticated California society. "They ate all organic foods, drank all kinds of wines, discussing every flavor endlessly, and then talked about saving whales and making gay marriage legal." She explained to Jake, "I think drinking Lone Star or Southern Comfort is just fine. I believe in equal rights for everyone but if anyone is gay in El Chico, they're not admitting to it."

Jake had nodded his head. "Of course no one would admit to being gay. It would be too hard to put up with the hatefulness from the holier-than-thou church ladies who have very long lists of what makes up being sinful. I might warn you, Bea, your visit to Las Vegas will rank high as a 'devil's don't', too."

"I know the church ladies don't like me much, Jake. But my whole life I've gone to First Methodist and I've tried to be a good Christian to everyone. With El Chico bein so small it's impossible to avoid the land mines of gossip spread by uptight, bored blabbermouths."

"You don't have much in common with them ladies. They don't understand you. Bea, you gotta realize that the Circle McP is a bigger business than most men run in this county."

"Yep. That's true. I guess I'm too outspoken and I know I don't like chitchat. I don't care what they say, I just cain't pass up this trip to Las Vegas."

Ding. Ding-ding-ding. Ding-ding-ding-ding. Click. Click-click. This was Bea's first glimpse of a real casino, a real Las Vegas casino. Her eyes were as big as when she was five and saw her first fireworks display at the Texas State Fair. Swaying in time with the upbeat music coming from the nearby lounge, she fingered her dress making sure it was in place. She gazed in wonder at the bright pulsating multicolored lights accentuated by the constant pulse of slot machines and voices encouraging lady luck to be theirs tonight. Bea could feel her heart pounding.

Harold bought Bea a ticket to Celine Dion's show. She was excited to see the star in person. Maybe she'd see other famous people walking around, like Blake Shelton or Tim McGraw. It was years too late to spot Frank Sinatra and the Rat Pack or Liberace, but she might see Wayne Newton.

Bea took the carpeted stairs into the pit of the casino. Harold and a group of friends had taken off to play blackjack. She wasn't confident she would be able to count to twenty-one fast enough to keep up, so she wandered. A group lined up chips on a table in front of the big Wheel of Fortune. The casino employee spun it, took piles of chips from the losers and shoved a few towards a young man who won. "I might play that game," she thought. "I guess I could pick a number and see if it wins. Seems kinda boring."

She followed a marble path to a large section of craps tables. She knew that's what they were from the Vegas television show and the brochure. After watching the excited betting, yelling, dice-throwing and more yelling she decided to keep moving. "Too complicated."

Bea liked watching the little white ball spin around the roulette wheel. "No matter how long I watch this, I cain't figure out the betting system." She continued around the casino gawking at the lavish décor, still looking for at least one celebrity.

Bea's feet felt like a cow had stomped on them. She knew the gold spike heels she ordered from Macy's catalogue were a tight fit, but they looked so nice with the skinny black dress she hadn't returned them.

She sank down on a stool next to a slot machine. Several happy-looking ladies sat in comfort playing the games. They punched buttons and the machines would click and jingle and play festive electronic melodies. Some of the women cheered when the displays indicated they'd won. Bea could see them grab ticket stubs generated by their machines. They'd go to the cashier's desk and leave with a stack of bills. That would suit her just fine.

She asked one of the Grecian goddesses with a drink-filled tray how to get started as a slot machine player. After brief instructions, Bea took five twenties out of her purse, the amount she set aside for Las Vegas gambling, went to the cashier and got cash cards.

She popped one into a slot. The bright display showed a big $20.00. Bea pushed a button and watched the dials spin around and around, finally stopping one at a time showing a king, then an eight, a four, a jack and a two. The display flashed $19.00, the balance left from her lost bet. She played again and again until the machine read $0.00. She inserted another card. When she got three nines in a row, her balance went up to $25.00 "This is fun!"

The lady next to her selected a bet of $5.00, so Bea followed her lead risking the five dollars she won. Once again she pressed the button and watched the dials as they flashed rows of cards. First, a ten of spades, then a king of spades, then a queen of spades. Click, click-click. A jack of spades!

"Oh my God!" the lady next to her shouted. "You might win." Click, click-click, click, CA-CHING!

Bells and whistles drowned out all other casino sounds. The Ace of Spades joined the lineup. A siren blasted. Security guards in red uniforms surrounded Bea. A Grecian goddess dropped her tray. People from all over the casino were running to see what happened. Harold appeared from nowhere and gave her a big hug in front of everyone. "This is my sister!" he screamed.

The next thing Bea knew she was shaking hands with the Casino boss. She had her photo taken, was handed a poster sized check and a lifetime pass to stay at the Bellagio. Bea won the Casino's Top Dollar Triple Gold Jackpot.

Harold's accountants helped Bea place more than a million dollars in securities and a smaller amount was sent back home to her El Chico bank account. No one but Harold knew exactly how much she won, not even Jake.

"The trip was like a picture show and I was the star," she explained to Jake as they sipped ice cold Lone Star on her porch. "The money's enough to keep the ranch goin."

The cowboy smiled and listened as Bea told about her big win.

"I had such fun. Mary Alice, Ally, took me shopping and I bought a real Las Vegas styled outfit." Bea showed Jake the silk blouse printed with playing cards and dice. Right on the front was a big ace of spades. "I'll keep this forever and show it off at my next Tech reunion, but probably not to the Methodist Ladies."

Jake laughed, "Nope, I guess not to the church ladies."

THE LADIES

News of Bea McPherson's good luck traveled fast once Marjorie Plunker, President of the El Chico Lady's Guild, heard about it from her bank president husband. Rarely had anyone from the town visited Las Vegas, and no one won anything major of any kind for as long as anyone in the small west Texas town could remember.

As Wilmur White, owner of the General Mercantile Store reported to local shoppers, "Sure, just about everyone buys a few lottery tickets on payday but so far we have no big winners except for Henry Logan. He won twenty-five dollars, but being the town drunk, he spent it in one fell swoop on Jack Daniels."

Marjorie informed her best friends, Minnie Lee Gibbons and Etta Ruth Foremost. "We simply must honor Bea with a party now that her bank balance is one of the biggest in town. It's become a necessity for local society to embrace her in spite of her, uhhhh, personality."

Marjorie's voice surged across her formal dining table set with Big Chief tablets, pens, and refreshments. Looking like a crane, long neck surrounded by a lace collar, she turned her head, swallowed and tucked a stray strand of gray hair into the tight bun at the back of her head "Will the meeting of the Bea Celebration Party Committee please come to order?"

Like Etta Ruth, Marjorie's lineage could be traced to the founding of El Chico. Her great-grandparents settled on government land as ranchers, passing it along to her grandparents. Her father continued ranching and oil was found on their acreage. This made her family one of the most prosperous in the county. She married Lester right out of high school. Their son was born seven months later and explained as a premature birth in spite of his eight-pound birth weight. At first the young family lived in the attic rooms of her parent's huge brick home but once they passed away, Marjorie inherited the residence, cementing her place in El Chico high society.

"Oh, Marjorie. You don't have to be so formal. There's just the three of us," Minnie Lee interjected.

Etta Ruth, grabbing another cookie off the refreshment plate and gulping some Diet Coca Cola added, "What's the big deal about honorin Bea McPherson, anyway? We never liked her. She's not proper."

In defense, Marjorie extended her neck and stuck her nose further in the air. "We haven't had a party in months. Everyone is tired of scrounging for water or a bit of coolness and Bea, bless her heart, is as good a reason as any to celebrate."

"She dresses a bit wild for my taste always wearing those tight jeans. You ought to see her at the Guild Ladies' meetings," said Minnie Lee.

"Well, now that she's as rich as all get-out, Jesus might change Bea." Etta Ruth still munched and sipped.

"You always said you couldn't figure out why anyone would live by themself surrounded by nothin but livestock and I've always thought it odd that cowhand, Jake, lives on her property. However, I do agree it's time for a party." After some rummaging, Minnie Lee retrieved an address book from her large handbag.

Etta Ruth, rotating her butterball neck and fanning, raised her hand, "I volunteer to be in charge of the refreshments committee. I'll make everyone's favorite, my Oreo Cake, the one I made for the church bazaar." Writing the menu on her tablet, she continued, "Minnie Lee, you can make the Hawaiian punch with the fruit ice float and Marjorie you can make the Onion Dip with chips."

"Because my house is one of the prettiest in town, not that I'm braggin, I volunteer to have the party here. Usually my yard is brimmin over with roses. Even in this dry spell I still have a few we can use for decorations. We'll be able to make the place look as festive as Founder's Day." Marjorie glowed as she spoke to Minnie Lee and Etta Ruth.

Minnie clapped her hands, "That's the perfect theme, 'Roses.' There's nothin like roses. However, I do want to mention one thing." Her voice lowered to a whisper. "I don't think we want to bring up the Las Vegas thing too much, just that we are honorin one of our fellow citizens who traveled afar and returned prosperous."

Etta Ruth stretched her chunky arms over her head attempting to get cool. "I hope she doesn't insist on wearing that awful fake-silk blouse covered with dice and playing cards. And, bless her heart, surely she can control that fuzzy red hair for one day."

Marjorie raised her voice gaining control of the meeting. "This all just sounds wonderful. We can have the party Saturday afternoon at two o'clock the week after next." Minnie Lee and Etta Ruth nodded in confirmation. "Then it's agreed. I'll write it down in my notes. I have invitations next on my list – they're like decorations – so that will be your job," Marjorie pointed to Minnie Lee.

When Marjorie called Bea to inform her she was to be the honored guest at a party, a shocked Bea tried to decline agreeing only after Marjorie persisted.

Looking at her dog, Bea frowned. "Buster, this means getting my hair done and drivin into town two extra times. I guess we'll live through it." She scratched behind his large floppy ears. "Why in the very hell would these three busybodies plan a party for me? They must be bored out of their gourds."

Meanwhile, the Bea Celebration Party Committee members scurried around addressing invitations, grocery shopping, and baking, getting ready for the big event. They called each other several times a day to discuss who had RSVP'd, and what to wear.

Buster was by Bea's side, his tail wagging and tongue hanging out as they walked to and from the mailbox. "Look here, big guy, a pink envelope! Jeez Louise, it's really beautiful." She tore it open. "See the big rose on this invitation with my name front and center? Roses have always been my favorite. I almost believe they want to include me in their social lives."

She chuckled, "It says I am returning from a long holiday out of state. I guess that's the way they describe four days in Las Vegas. I can hardly wait to tell the ladies about winning the Jackpot and about the casinos and gambling. This will give them something to talk about for a long time." Buster yawned.

On the day of the celebration Bea took an especially long bath, practically draining the well. She used her favorite Yardley English Rose bath crystals and spritzed all over with rose cologne. Buster sneezed and shook his head.

Taking special care to keep her curls in order, Bea slipped on the red skirt and silk blouse she bought in Vegas. She struggled into the gold high heels and hugged Buster goodbye.

"I'll see you in time for supper," she said climbing into her big, white Cadillac Escalade with the CircleMcP license plate purchased with part of her winnings.

The party home was filled with rose arrangements in crystal vases. The table was set with Marjorie's antique rose china accessorized with matching rose paper napkins and tablecloth carefully selected at Walmart. The room freshener and candles were rose scented, as was the soap in the powder room. The Oreo Cake was topped with fresh roses and petals were sprinkled from the front porch to the dining room.

Bea arrived a fashionable ten minutes after two, walking slowly up the sidewalk, proceeding carefully up the front steps of the big old Victorian house. She knocked. Marjorie, Minnie Lee, and Etta Ruth swung open the door.

"Hello," they chimed, "do come in. The ladies are in the parlor. "

"Let me pin your corsage on," said Marjorie. "I took corsage makin last fall at the high school adult education class and mine looks almost as good as those from Elma's Florist Shop, don't you think?"

As Bea's heels clip-clopped on the wood floor, the hostesses looked at each other, rolled their eyes, and whispered.

"I told you she had no class," said Minnie Lee.

"And, look at that outfit!" hissed Etta Ruth.

"The other ladies are having such a great time, they won't even notice her," Marjorie added.

The chitchatting crowd turned as Bea entered the parlor. The guests gathered around the honoree, had her sit in a large Queen Anne chair, and asked to hear all about her trip to Las Vegas.

Like a flock of birds, the women twittered, "We saw your picture and the article on the front page of the *El Chico Times Gazette* yesterday. How exciting! When did you get back? Did you see any stars? What was it like to win and what will you do with all that money?"

They oooooed and ahhhhhhhed about her outfit, telling her how great she looked. Bea was delighted. She told them all about getting her picture made with the casino boss, and about the musical water fountains at Bellagio's. Bea was a celebrity.

Later that day she sat on the ranch's front porch sipping iced tea with Jake. Bea told the foreman about her party and the kind reception she received from most of El Chico's women. Then she giggled. "You should have seen Marjorie, Minnie Lee, and Etta Ruth when the other ladies made a big fuss over me and the article in the paper. They were almost speechless. Bless their hearts."

Jake rolled back in his chair, sipped his drink and snickered, "Yeah. Bless their hearts."

ED

When entering El Chico's city limits from the south, the first sign of life was Ed's. An enormous Texas flag flew high on a pole cemented into a wall made of iridescent silica rock from the old glass factory kiln. A large sign mounted at the side of the shiny Airstream Ed used as his office announced Ed's Main Street Salvage Company and Golf Course in bold red letters.

A person passing through the little town might see the stocky man dressed in western boots, jeans and a starched shirt sorting through his treasures. Ed Hawkins lived his entire life in El Chico, son of a glass factory worker and a homemaker in the old tradition. He and his wife, Odelia, were always sweethearts. He had been a star football player for the Horn Toad team and she, a cheerleader. They married right out of high school, had two daughters, and never considered life could be lived anywhere but in El Chico.

It pleased Ed that Odelia was still one of the prettiest women around. Her long auburn hair was the same color with only a few strands of gray and her figure was almost as slender and curvy as when she was twenty. She quickly defended her man in public, but at home she was just as swift to express a differing opinion if she thought he was out of line. Odelia volunteered at the library two days a week and both she and Ed read just about every book on its shelves. Each evening the couple shared several paragraphs of whatever they were reading, educating themselves about life outside their little Utopia.

Nothing got Ed more riled up than when folks used the words, "junk" to describe the ten acres of prized objects making up his business inventory. His salvaged goods ranged from tiny screws to vats the size of small buildings. These things were of genuine value to large Houston foundries that shopped his place once or twice a year. The collection included an assortment of auto parts dating back to the early days of the automobile.

"Don't know why every one of these hubcaps and hood ornaments hasn't sold. Anyone with the sense of a snake can see the valueability of quality chrome. I bet some of these ought to be in a museum somewhere." Ed muttered to himself as he added a few recent acquisitions to the display covering the wall of his storage shed and the length of fence facing the highway.

The El Chico native continued around his property organizing sheet metal according to size, shape and thickness. Each product line was displayed in easy-to-see rows and bins. The salvage company kept Ed, Odelia Marie and their two girls living comfortably in a neat, yellow-painted, wood-frame home. It was nice, even if their view included stacks of unattractive second-hand goods.

Ed bragged to friends and customers that everything he owned was bought cheap and sold as bargains. He had what he liked to think of as a super instinct for value and a remarkable ability to make a good deal. When a business closed or a building was torn down, he was the first in line to buy things other people overlooked.

For example, when the town's hospital closed some fifteen years earlier he filled up a corner of his property with medical equipment. He bought all the ancient metal beds for practically nothing. Odelia was not happy that he insisted on using some of them in their own home, but Ed saw the advantage of having a bed that could be cranked up and down for reading and such. "All they need is a little orl on them hinges," he told his wife.

When part of the San Marcos Cotton Gin and Fabric Factory went out of business, Ed returned home with his pickup piled high with Singer Sewing Machines and bolts of cotton fabrics. Because of that purchase, most El Chico homes had matching decorative themes that included homemade flowered or plaid cotton curtains, bedspreads and cushions. Ethel Ogletree made interchangeable bands for some of her hats and Annie Adams made her daughter's bridesmaids' dresses out of pink, flowered organza Ed sold at a discount.

Two years before Ed admitted, but only to himself, that he was bored. "The girls have married and gone on to live in Dallas and Austin. Odelia's busy with the church and her sewing circle. All I do is sort and re-sort inventory, day after day." To pass the time, Ed took naps, ate snacks and got in the habit of watching the Oprah Channel each afternoon in his Airstream office. One day he listened as Dr. Oz talked about males and their medical challenges. Ed was glued to the show, learning how men enter a new, less-sexy phase in their lives around his age. These men, maybe even Ed himself, needed new interests, something to keep them from turning into grumpy old codgers.

As Ed sorted rusty lawn furniture parts, he pondered what the good doctor said. Making his way to the where his property met the town cemetery, he opened crates purchased from Continental Airline's annual lost luggage sale, always a fun project. The first container was filled with ladies' clothes and makeup. He'd give that to the churchwomen to help the poor, knowing he'd soon see Odelia and her friends using most of it themselves.

Ed strained as he opened the second Continental crate and laughed out loud when he saw the contents, "I've hit pay dirt, by damn!" He pulled out dusty leather golf bags filled with clubs and dozens of balls. He grabbed a club and took a swing. Remembering Dr. Oz's advice, he moved a pile of hubcaps, bumpers and wheels. "Maybe I could take up the game."

Ed spent the afternoon hitting golf balls; first over the pile of golf bags, then aiming at various points around the yard. For the next few mornings he bounced out of bed anxious to continue his golfing. He moved a huge pile of bricks, remainders of the old hospital beds, and some car parts, creating a long clear space. As he practiced, his aim and enthusiasm for the sport improved.

For a week he shoved, moved and reorganized his great

collection. He selected a child's playhouse, a dump truck bed and an old plow as interesting features to use.

He created a makeshift fairway where his property went slightly up hill with three big cottonwoods on the right side. He embellished it with hospital bed headboards and Model T running boards. After all, they did look a bit like a fence. To create a green, he smoothed the ground, covered it with some Astroturf he got when the Astrodome closed and put a hole in the middle.

"Since golf is Scottish and the Scots like plaid, this might work." He gazed at a triangular scrap of plaid cotton fabric as sweat poured off his thinning hairline and down his forehead. He placed the new flag on top of an IV pole and stuck it in the ground. "Another bargain from the hospital demolition! And to think Odelia questioned that purchase."

That's when he knew he could make a move as impressive as a hole in one.

At supper that night, Ed shared his idea. "Odelia, El Chico has no golf course, so I got to thinkin, I'll invent one right on our property."

"And I thought you were finally cleanin up the place! But no, you've most assuredly lost your mind thinkin folks here are going to want to hit that little ball around the salvage yard." Odelia shouted.

"This here's gonna make me young again, Odelia Marie. You jus wait an see!

The next afternoon, Chester Cartwright and Doug Farnsworth came by for their regular game of Forty-two. "What in the hell are you up to, Ed? Looks like a tornado come through. You ain't goin out of business, are you?" asked Doug.

"Nope. Dr. Oz, the TV doctor, says it's good to do somethin different. I'm in a new phase of my life."

"You ain't takin up a new church group are you? Odelia is gonna be kinda mad." Chester gazed at the kidney-shaped piece of Astroturf.

"I said, 'phase', not 'praise', stupid. I'm tryin somethin I ain't done before to keep my juices alive so I won't be a cantankerous ol man like you. I'm playin golf. Maybe not like that Tiger Woods fellow, but it's golf all the same," defended Ed.

With that, he led his two friends out to the fairway. He handed each a club and a ball and they spent the rest of the day swinging and laughing and joking. By that night Ed had some partners to help with the project.

For the next few months Ed and Doug moved the debris while Chester and his bulldozer moved the land creating pathways and small hills around the rubbish. Other friends joined in the work, ending their days hitting balls around what served El Chico as a golf course.

Seeing the men enthusiastic about doing something for the first time in years, Odelia persuaded her sewing circle to join in, bringing rakes, seeds and flowers to landscape the new course. They put plants in every container they found, from washer insides to toilet bowls. Ed mounted fan blades and flags on top of a derrick to show wind direction. Vats, once used for milk storage, were sunk in the ground and transformed into water traps.

Bea McPherson's new gossip column in the *El Chico Times Gazette* featured Ed's Golf Course, which became the talk of the town. Ed helped Lulu Belle Schwartz order closeout golf shirts to sell in her boutique and Coach Neighbors began plans for a golf team.

That's when Ed added the words *and Golf Course* to his *Ed's Salvage Yard* sign.

FARNSWORTH'S

Somewhere between Houston and Lubbock truckers saw the sawed-off mountain in the distance, warning them to downshift for the stop up ahead. They knew Dalton Darnell, El Chico's Sheriff, would be waiting to see if they stopped dead still at the red blinking traffic light, the one they believed the town council put there to slow the big eighteen-wheelers and encourage the turn in Farnsworth's Truck Stop and Cafe. Wilma's homemade pies made up for the inconvenience.

Juan Martinez and Big Al Mosley pulled out of Farnsworth's. They had filled their big rig's tank with diesel and their bellies with genuine Texas Beef Burgers followed by pie. Big Al preferred lemon meringue, and Juan, apple-peach when it was in season.

The Farnsworth family lived behind the truck stop in a nice doublewide mobile home, complete with a front porch Doug added in the late 80s, when they first settled in the small town. It was convenient to live where they could watch the business and their boy at the same time. Joe had real musical talent from when he was tiny, able to pick up almost any instrument and perfect tunes within days. When he was twelve he started writing his own music and on his nineteenth birthday he and his guitar left El Chico for Nashville. He became a local hero when he hooked up with Lyle Lovett's band making a name for himself in country music.

A few years earlier, Doug found an almost dead puppy on the highway right where the big eighteen-wheelers turn in. "Wilma, it's a wonder the tiny mongrel wasn't run over and squashed flat as a tortilla."

She took him in and nursed him around the clock with warm milk and gravy, creating a bond that only a dog has with its person.

From the beginning, he never strayed far from Wilma's side. The pup gave her moral support as she cooked or did the business paperwork. When she went into town, he perched on the front seat of the Ford truck and waited patiently while she ran errands.

The big creature was friendly to all the truckers, meeting them with his long, lab-like wagging tail, nuzzling their hands with his pointed German Shepherd nose, and indicating his need for a scratch behind his drooping basset ears. His coat was curly and coffee-colored, except for the white triangle on his chest. He was a real hodge-podge of a dog and that was his name.

Doug closed the café in the evenings by ten, in time to join Wilma and Hodge for the Abilene news on TV. They left the station and pumps open for late customers on the honor system. Most used credit cards so Doug didn't have to be there.

On the night Hodge-Podge got a new name, Doug heard the buzzer announcing a truck was fueling up. It buzzed over and over so he left the house and sauntered up to the small station office to see what was going on. That's when he was grabbed from behind and felt a gun thrust into the side of his head.

"Okay, now. Where's the cash?" A low voice growled.

Doug pointed to the cash register, "I'll get it for you. Don't panic."

"Don't give me orders," said the man as he shoved Doug towards the money.

About then, a second, larger guy appeared. "I don't see anyone else around, but I turned off the sign to be sure no one stops."

Doug opened the register and shoved a few bills towards them. "Take it and go."

"Not so easy, Mr. Farnsworth," said the larger guy. "We want the rest of it, the stash. We know you have lots more cash around than this."

Both guys smirked. Pointing the gun in Doug's face, the first man said, "Shut up and take us to the back! Your house."

The three of them rounded the café and stepped onto the porch. Hodge started barking and bounded out the door. Doug yelled as loud as he could, "Run, Wilma, Run!" The gun went off in Hodge's direction. Doug went down when the butt of the gun hit the side of his head. The next thing he knew, he was on the couch and Wilma was sitting beside him.

"Don't worry, Doug. I'm okay," said Wilma with tears streaming down her cheeks. "But I think he shot Hodge. He yelped and went runnin."

"Shut up!" screamed the first man. "You ain't gonna believe the hurt we'll give you if you don't hand over the money." His partner was tearing the place apart, slinging books and dishes across the room.

"I promise there's no more. Wilma went to the bank today. We only keep enough for change."

The next ten minutes were a nightmare. "Undress! Yeah, and I mean it, down to nothing."

The culprits threw Wilma and Doug onto the floor and tied them up. They kicked and hit the couple with the pistol over and over again. Wilma was no longer crying. She was passed out, or dead, Doug didn't know which. He fought to get out of the ropes with no luck.

Then he heard loud barking. It was Hodge and he was running up and down the front porch. The first robber opened the door with his gun blazing and then fell forward, right onto his face. Suddenly the house filled with Highway Patrolmen. Sheriff Dalton Darnell pointed his gun at the second intruder and cuffed him all in one motion.

Hodge-Podge was licking Wilma's face and whimpering. Her eyes fluttered open and she managed a smile. Both Doug and Wilma were covered with blankets and untied. Doc Wilson, the town vet and only medical person in town, appeared with his black bag administering first aid to the couple while waiting for an ambulance to arrive from the county seat.

"Please watch over Hodge while we're away," said Wilma to the vet. "And have everyone help themselves in the café."

When questioned by the sheriff, the two intruders told the whole story. They were each on parole, so were drifting around Texas doing odd jobs. "One night we heard a big guy with fancy boots over in Dallas talkin about the Farnsworths. He said their son was a big Nashville star in Lyle Lovett's Band. This fellow told us the Farnsworth's didn't believe in banks and kept all the family money at their truck stop. He bought us beers and told us it would be real easy pickens for anyone who knew anything about robberies. So, we decided we'd try for some quick cash. We had no idea we'd be bamboozled by a damn mutt."

Within an hour, a parade of truckers, a few townspeople and the State Patrolmen sat around the café eating burgers and pie as they discussed the evening's events.

The group quizzed Sheriff Darnell as he fed Hodge a burger. "It seems as soon as this old guy knew there was trouble, he took off runnin to my house. I heard the barkin, got up from my TV watchin and saw Hodge-Podge. I knew there was trouble when he was there without Wilma. He was barkin and runnin up and down the road towards home."

A Highway Patrol officer continued the story as he passed a basket around for donations to aid the couple and pay for the burgers. "We got a call from the Sheriff and rushed to the scene."

Wiping a piece of meringue from his lips, Dalton continued the tale. "The front lights were off and Doug never turns the lights out, so I knew for sure somethin bad was goin down. I followed Hodge around back to their house and looked through a window. Doug and Wilma were tied up on the floor, all bloody and passed out. By then the State Patrol guys were here and we surrounded the place. Hodge started barkin and the suspects heard him. When the first one came out the door, I hit him on the head, bringing him down like I was Walker, Texas Ranger."

"We entered the house and apprehended the second man. Now both are on their way to the county jail," added a patrolman, mouth full of pie. "They'll be put away for a long time. This was armed robbery and maybe even attempted murder."

Doc Wilson, who had taken Wilma's place at the grill, finished stacking a plate with burgers, "I did what I could for the Farnworths until the ambulance and medics got here from the county hospital. They were in pretty bad shape, but their injuries didn't look life threatening. This here dog saved them from those SOBs."

Rigs were still pulling up in front of the truck stop cafe. It looked like every trucker from Amarillo to Dallas heard the CB buzz.

Leaning down, Big Al, from Patton Trucking, scratched the dog behind his ear. "I heard the Sheriff on the radio and put out a call, 'Stand on it and boogie to Farnsworth's, bears need help.'"

Juan Martinez, Al's partner, chimed in. "Listen up everybody." Setting the dog on a table, he toasted him with a Coke, "You're no Hodge-Podge, you're a big hero. All the drivers think you need a new handle. We're callin you Ten-Four from now on, cause you're A-OK."

A week later, Wilma and Doug were out of the hospital and back at work. Both had serious bruises, lots of stitches, but no broken bones. Joe came home, followed by the band, to make sure his parents were all right. They played a free concert at the On the Road Again Bar & Grill and the entire town turned out. At Wilma's insistence, Clarajean sang a couple of songs impressing Lyle with her talent and Joe with her charm. So, what started as a bad situation turned into a celebration for El Chico.

The hero-dog was featured on the front page of the *El Chico Times Gazette*. The Dallas papers picked it up, scattering the news nationally. NBC News sent a crew to Farnsworth Corner (the media's term) to interview Joe and his parents with Ten-Four by their side swishing his big tail and grinning from one long, droopy ear to the other.

"Nick, what did you mean telling two fellows to come rob the

Farnsworths?" The Mayor was distressed when he heard about the robbery and how the two culprits got the lead on the job. Putting facts together he figured out the man in the bar wearing fancy boots had to be Nick.

"Oh now, Percy. I didn't tell those two dummies to rob the Farnsworths. They decided that all by themselves, but, having a little crime out at Farnsworth's Truck Stop might get the couple to sell out. It's a piece of property we need." Graystone leaned back in his chair as he talked to Percy on the phone.

"Well, partner, I'm afraid your plan backfired. All they got was good publicity so now they've got a slew of visitors wanting Wilma's pies and a look at that stupid hound."

CITY COUNCIL

A week later, after a few cups of Maryland Club coffee and two boxes of doughnuts, the six council members lined up in chairs waiting to hear a formal presentation by none other than Mr. Nicholas Graystone. He arrived early that morning from Dallas, following the plan he and the mayor devised.

The town council's meeting was taking place in the "highrise" parlor atop the town's tallest building. The three-story brick cube was the newest structure for miles around. The mayor himself had spearheaded the project, finding the land and fast-talking some Houston investors, relatives of older locals, into funding the senior residences. A huge sales campaign managed by Etta had filled the place with seven affluent retirees from the area, freeing up five large homes and two ranches, inventory for the good mayor to sell through his real estate business.

Unknown to anyone but his wife, Percy bought and rented out all but one of the homes under the name of a company he formed for just such purposes. He also purchased part of a ranch property that backed up to the motel and base of the mountain, putting cash in his pocket from the sale of the remaining land. Even then, before he met Graystone, he knew owning El Chico property would one day pay off big-time.

The large man stood in front of the council, his presence crowding the small room. He wore tailored jeans and a black belt with a custom designed sterling silver buckle. His shirt, opened at the neck, was white, set off by black pearl snaps. Graystone's boots were black leather with a single white star on the toes. "First of all I want to thank you for havin me." When he saw Bea in the back corner taking notes, he took a deep breath and, with a wider than usual grin said, " I am fallin in love with your town, its beauty and warm hospitality."

He took another deep breath and refocused on his mission. "Today I'm here to give you the results of the feasibility study and to propose a project I believe will go a long way in saving El Chico. My company, The H₂O Engineering Firm, suggests constructing a pipeline of 12-inch PVC from the County Reservoir to El Chico, with the goal of providing the water needed to sustain your town."

Once again, he displayed an array of charts, graphs and drawings. Graystone aimed a laser pointer at a blueprint showing a maze of pipes and a map with official looking lines going here and there "And, you'll see how the up and down flow over the hilly terrain will be aided by a series of pumps at points a, b, c, and d."

He continued his presentation, detailing the scheme. "The water would flow to a tower receptacle set on the side of El Chico Mountain and replace your current rusted-out tank and pump. This grand tower would not only hold water, but would be a powerful addition to the skyline of your lovely little city."

"So you're proposin we hire your firm to bring the water seventy miles? How would you get rights-of-way permissions to do that? And why would anyone in West Texas give up any of their valuable water?" A puzzled Ed Hawkins scratched his head.

"Those are good questions, Mr. Hawkins. Question one. I assure you my firm is well equipped to handle legalities. We've done it many times before. Once funds are allocated, H₂O Engineering will secure the rights-of-way and begin work on a six-foot deep trench to house the actual pipeline. Question two. Your neighbors over in Ivie will be glad to sell a little of their water to help raise funds for their new underground storage facility. We will not impact their inventory to any degree."

The mayor stepped forward. "Nick, tell them about the ASRs."

"What's ASRs?" Lester Plunker asked.

Graystone smiled. "I am glad you asked. This is the newest

solution to water shortage in the country and what I propose for El Chico. Aquifer Storage and Recovery. Most of above ground reservoir water is lost by evaporation in hot climates like we have in Texas. ASR is a method for gathering the surface water and pumping it down into existing aquifers for storage thus preventing the massive loss due to evaporation. Like here in El Chico, the water would be directed by the pipeline to the aquifer and then pumped, as needed, into your tower and eventually distributed."

"I don't see any reports about possibly drillin for water deeper in our aquifer. Did you research that option?" Ed was bewildered.

"I assure you there's not enough water there to drill for." Graystone pointed to Herb Matson, wanting to change the subject.

"If I understand you and these figures, we would need to assess each property owner a tax increase of six percent over their current rate," said Herb Matson, flipping through the stack of papers Graystone had passed out to each attendee.

Lester Plunker, thinking of the dwindling deposits in his bank, stood up. "Like Herb, I wonder how our little town could afford such an expensive project."

The mayor joined the engineer at the front of the room. "We still have some figurin to do on the exact amount, but, yes, we will have to increase taxes and start collections soon."

The Dallasite again smiled at Bea who frowned at him as she took notes. "I know this sounds like a lot when your town's economy is down, but with what's at stake and what the potential outcome of having abundant water in the area will mean to each citizen, no sacrifice should be too great. Just think what it will be like when a booming economy returns to El Chico."

Graystone looked around the room at the doubtful faces and continued his pitch. "This is a lot to deal with. However, the water tower itself will add a new dimension to El Chico. It would be a beacon to people approaching your fair city; could be seen for miles around. Maybe, a nice touch would be placing a replica of your championship team's mascot on top of the tower." The council members murmured among themselves and smiled at the mention of the Horn Toads.

"I like that idea. The Horn Toads have always been important to the region. When the stadium fills up on Friday nights we all do more business." Ed Hawkins smiled as he pictured customers stopping at the Salvage Yard.

"Now, that's good thinkin, Mr. Hawkins. With that kind of attitude I'm sure you'll be able to accomplish the tax increase easily over time. I suggest collecting a base amount now, and then assessing the balance over the next few years. According to Percy, you could start construction on the water tower right away out of current funds."

"Nick, that sounds like a working plan to me," said the mayor winking at his secret partner. "Just leave us a bill for the study H2O conducted and we'll send you a check. Meanwhile, I believe you've given our council enough information. Once we go over all the data we'll be able to make a decision on this worthwhile project and we'll get together again. This is the wise choice if we don't want to lose all we've developed in our little piece of Texas."

"Well, then. I'll thank you for your hospitality." Graystone gathered his papers, placed them in the now-familiar western-tooled brief case. "If you have any questions about details, Percy can reach me anytime. I'll provide quick answers." He waved and smiled as he left the council. He tipped his Stetson and winked as he took a final glance at Bea McPherson.

After a break for more doughnuts and coffee, the council reconvened, reading through the stack of papers a page at a time.

A grimacing Lester Plunker stood up and spoke. "Many folks are out of work because the cattle business has gone to hell in a hand-basket. The citizen's bank accounts are evaporating as fast as the water supply. I don't see how we can pass a tax increase on El Chico's people. Plus, an increase on poor folks doesn't help a bit. They pay nothing in taxes. Nothin added to nothin adds up to nothin for fundraising revenues."

"I agree. Some people are so poor I know they're buying dog food for themselves, not their dogs," said Wilmur White, owner of the grocery store. I try to extend credit but I'm at the point I can't pay for my own inventory."

"The truck stop is doin okay with all our recent publicity, but still not as good as it used to before this heat wave. Whatever we do, I think the town needs somethin to look forward to, somethin to give them hope for the future," added Doug Farnsworth, "and higher taxes won't do it."

"What if Silver Crow and his people can get us water?" Ed Hawkins looked at his fellow council members one at a time. "I volunteer the back acre of the salvage yard for the ceremony."

"Oh bullshit, Ed! Injun rain dancin and painted faces jumpin up and down, that's old fashioned legend stuff," said the mayor

"Marjorie and all the church ladies would never see fit to let some non-Christian heathens lead the city in a rain dance. So, that's out for sure," added the bank president, whose henpecking wife was the Church Lady's Guild president.

The mayor's face turned red, his voice got louder and he pulled hard on his mustache. "This water pipeline'll work and it'll save our town. Nick's team can have it installed with a minimal tax increase and El Chico will have water in two short years. That will bring back the cattle business and then everyone will have jobs and money."

After a long silence, the always-resourceful Ed Hawkins stood and spoke to the group. "I might be able to find us a salvaged water tower somewhere. We could restore it and install it ourselves with only a little professional help."

"I do think the pipeline would work and maybe some of the rich folks in town would pay more taxes, chip in for the greater good." Oliver Brumfeld, El Chico's resident bachelor, spoke in his high-pitched voice, sounding like nails scraping across a blackboard. Clearning his throat, he added, "I most definitely like the idea of a water tower. It would be a nice architectural feature for El Chico, don't you think? It would be an inspiration to everybody for miles around." He gazed off into the distance. "I can see it now, at the side of the mountain, rising 150 feet into the sky."

Herb Matson, town treasurer, removed his glasses. "I've run the numbers for a new tower and it won't be smart to use that much of our money. But, if Ed can find us a used one, we might make it work."

The mayor pounded his gavel, "I think we all agree that Nick's idea of mounting a big fiberglass replica of the mascot on top of the tower is a great one. We could write, 'El Chico Fighting Horn Toads' across the side. I say let's go for it."

Bea McPherson stood and raised her voice, unable to hold her temper a minute longer. "Are y'all nuts? I know I'm only the secretary, but I've heard enough. We're talkin about water and survival here. This isn't a high-school pep rally. First of all, you **heard** a lot of us can barely afford to put food on the table! Second, we need to check out this Nicholas Graystone, his engineers, and whether the idea of piping water would even work."

The councilmen looked like a group of little leaguers who just lost their game.

"But, Nick knows everyone in Dallas. Just imagine working with an Aggie-ex-Dallas Cowboy. I'm sure a hero like Nick can be trusted to get the water we need," the Mayor added defensively.

Ed's stomach growled so loud it interrupted the argument. Bea stood, a figure to be reckoned with. Her western shirt was tucked into low cut jeans. The hand-tooled belt, emphasized by the state championship barrel-racing buckle, still fit twenty years after retirement from competition. With all eyes on her, she said, "Boys, I think it's time for lunch. Let's discuss this at next Wednesday's meetin."

"But, but, what if Nick changes his mind about helping us?" whined the mayor.

"What if the sky falls? What if Martians land?" Bea turned and walked out the door looking like a rock star followed by a crowd of awestruck groupies, as she lead the town fathers down the street and across the highway to the On the Road Again Bar and Grill.

CHURCH

It was well over a hundred degrees outside and the two window-mounted air conditioning units didn't make a dent in the sweltering weather that came right through the little church's red brick facade. Only a few faithful parishioners endured both the temperature and boring sermon.

The Reverend Isaiah P. (for Paul) Pevey stood front and center before the El Chico Methodist Church, perched on a raised platform just as he had every Sunday for the year he'd been in El Chico. In spite of the heat, the very short, very fat, very bald preacher wore a long black robe trimmed with crimson. He looked like a pool ball ready to roll into the rows of wooden pews. Brother Pevey was framed by a giant stained glass window depicting Christ with outstretched arms. The window was one of the town's treasures, made and donated by hardworking employees of the defunct glass factory.

The preacher spoke in his most professional baritone voice. "And hear my word … that is … er … God's word. Right here in our little community we have sinners, big sinners. Each of us is being judged at every moment. The Lord has seen our sins and has afflicted us with this drought. Our ground is cracking, turning to dust, just like WE will one day." His voice rose in a crescendo, startling the lulled congregation. "None of us knows when our time will come. It could be right on your way home, or when you are eating breakfast, or anytime. So, I beseech you, watch what you are doing. Are you carrying gossip along? Are you smoking those cigar-ettes? Are you lying? Are you drinking whiskey or fornicating?"

Sweat beaded on his forehead as he lowered his voice, hoping to sound like Christ would've sounded. He continued quoting from the Bible, waving it as high in the air as his short arms allowed. "Remember what the good book says. 'So, whoever knows the right thing to do and fails to do it, for him it is sin.' James 4:17, and 'For the wages of sin is death.' Romans 6:23. My friends, if you take the Lord into your heart today, 'you shall be like a watered garden, like a spring of water who waters fail not.' Isaiah 58:11."

With that, he laid his Bible on the podium, wiped his face with a handkerchief and lowered his head as if in deep prayer. "All you sinners wanting to repent today file to the front of the church. We can pray together for your soul right here and now. Brothers and Sisters, don't put it off another day, another hour, another minute. Jesus is waiting with open arms. Come now and your sins will be forgiven, put behind you and our drought will end. Amen."

On clue, his wife, Mabel, pounded the organ and *Onward Christian Soldiers* bellowed throughout the church and into the El Chico countryside. If someone had decided to enjoy a quiet Sunday at home, they'd get a dose of Christianity in spite of their wishes. They could not avoid the zealous efforts of the Methodists to recruit them as members of Jesus' family.

"Oh my, my, Brother Pevey, the sermon was magnificent," said Mary Nelle Matson, shaking the minister's sweaty hand as the crowd descended the steep stairway. Her head stacked high with brunette-tinted hair seemed to sit on the stiff collar of her starched white blouse. Her husband had scooted ahead of her, avoiding the preacher altogether.

"Herb, Herb, wait up," Mary Nelle crooned across the rocky parking lot. Holding her black patent purse in one hand and the hem of her long floral skirt in the other, she ran to catch up. In a whispered voice, not wanting to attract the attention of her fellow churchgoers, she scolded, "What in the world are you doin avoidin the preacher that way?"

He opened the door for his wife. His words were disjointed as he tried to hold his temper. Herb ripped his tie off and tossed it into the back seat of their Dodge Dart. "What a bag of hot air that man is, Mary Nelle. You drug me to church this week but I'm not goin again. What in the hell was he sayin about some sinner dying on the way home from church?"

"Don't cuss, Herb. Not on Sunday. Brother Pevey is an educated man and he can quote the scriptures like no one I've ever heard. You know he graduated from a college somewhere."

"And I guess that makes him know the Lord's intentions. He don't even know enough to stop being a glutton. You can see that from his big stomach. He's so fat I bet his wife has to tie his shoelaces for him," Herb laughed out loud at his joke.

He rolled his eyes as he drove two blocks up the gravel street and turned up the winding road at the base of the mountain to their small, neat frame house. "Mary Nelle, I keep the books for the church and will continue to, but don't ask any more of me when it comes to religion. Please."

Mary Nelle scowled as she opened her car door. Turning to look her husband in the eyes she barked, "Well, I invited him and the Mrs. to come over for supper after Wednesday night's service, so just get ready to be nice."

"Damn it, Mary Nelle. I've been baptized and I pray, why do I have to be friends with the minister. You act like that's gonna get us a free ticket to heaven."

Ethel Ogletree was leading the group in prayer when Mary Nelle arrived at Monday morning's Ladies Church Circle. Ethel's straw-hat-covered head was bowed and she was having trouble keeping her bifocals on her face as she swayed back and forth on her spike heels. "And Dear Lord, we ask that you hear us as we pray for wisdom in assembling the shoe box gifts for the dear little souls in darkest Africa, that these offerings will fulfill their needs for school supplies.

We heard your gracious word Sunday from the mouth of Preacher Pevey." Ethel consulted the paper in front of her, "So, 'whoever knows the right thing to do and fails to do it, for him it is sin.' James 4:17; and 'The wages of sin is death.' Romans 6:23, and 'You shall be like a watered garden, like a spring of water who waters fail not.' Isaiah 58:11. And, Lord, we do pray for rain and for forgiveness of our sins. Amen."

Ethel looked up and stared over her narrow glasses reminding Mary Nelle of the wide-eyed bass she cooked last night.

"We got started without you, Mary Nelle, just had to, so we can get all the boxes stuffed by the time Mario from the Post Office comes to pick them up."

"That's simply wonderful, everyone. I'm late for a very good reason." Mary Nelle placed a big plastic container on the floor. "As Chairman of the Foreign Mission Committee, I picked up this generous donation from Mr. White. He went through his storeroom and found these notebooks, pencils, and pens and said we could add them to the boxes. Even though he thinks the colored people in El Chico have overstepped their place, he supports the children in deepest Africa."

Marjorie and Etta Ruth rushed over to get the supplies, ooohing and ahhhing.

Bea, a new member of the group and always outspoken, jumped in front of them. "Wilmur White should be ashamed. Here he is a full deacon in the church and still not willing to love all people like Jesus taught us."

Ethel watched each of the women as they stuffed boxes. "Maybe Wilmur is the one mentioned in the sermon and we can get ready for him to die any day now."

"I say Wilmur has a good heart. But I do wonder just who Brother Pevey was citing as getting ready to kick the bucket due to sinning," said Mary Nelle. The chatter was deafening as the ladies discussed the sermon.

No one noticed Etta Ruth's hands shaking as she passed a tray of cookies around the group, fearing that she and the mayor should prepare for eminent demise.

"It might be Juanita Gutierrez over at the Dairy Queen with all those short skirts, low-cut blouses, and long hair. She is only a good witness for one thing. We all know what that is and it's not church." Marjorie rolled her eyes.

"Pardon me, ladies," said Bea standing up. "Like the good book says in another place, let's take a peek at ourselves first before staring at others to see who sins. Maybe being nice to Juanita would be more Christ-like than gossiping about her."

"Well, I think the preacher was trying to get somebody's attention and I wonder whose," said Etta Ruth with a worried frown on her face.

The group continued talking as they completed the boxes for shipment.

After the Wednesday night service, which consisted of more scripture readings and Bible-beating by the Reverend Pevey, he and his wife shared supper at the Matson's. To please Mary Nelle, Herb manufactured a smile and remained quiet except for occasional grunts and nods. He concentrated on the barbecued sausage, mashed potatoes, and cole slaw carefully prepared by his well-meaning spouse.

Once the minister and his wife drove away, Herb exploded. "This man is a real prize. I've never seen a human in my life able to gobble so much food and get so many words out of his mouth at the same time, none of them meaning anything. He could be an act at the county fair."

Mary Nelle giggled as she cleared the table and began washing the dishes. "I have to agree, Herb. I was afraid the dining room chair would break when he sat down. And, poor little Mabel, she didn't say hardly a word."

"I gave up tryin to understand the man thirty seconds into the visit. He seems to have set hisself up as Jesus Christ of El Chico. Like I said, you got me to church last week, but you won't see me there again."

Sunday morning Mary Nelle joined Ethel, Marjorie, Etta Ruth, and Bea in the third pew, left side of the church. The room was filled with the town's women plus a few henpecked husbands. They sat, quietly, fanning their faces with church programs waiting for the service to begin. The minutes passed, the heat getting more oppressive and the din becoming loud as folks discussed why the minister was late.

After what seemed like an hour, Lester Plunker appeared from the side door and with his head bowed, made his way to the front of the church. "I have some sad news today, brethren and sisters. Our minister, the Reverend Isaiah P. Pevey went to join our Lord last night. Mabel called to announce his passing and asked us to pray for his soul."

After a brief silence the shocked parishioners began to talk among themselves. Marjorie leaned over to the other ladies. "Well! Remember last week's sermon about a sinner and death? Now I guess we know who it was aimed at, don't we?"

No one noticed Etta Ruth's relieved expression. For the first time in a week, she felt calm. Maybe the Lord didn't consider taking advantage of neighbors a sin.

MUSIC

Mabel Pevey hummed "Happy Days are Here Again" as she twisted her long gray hair into a bun at the back of her head. She dabbed on some pale pink lipstick and put on her black gabardine dress, the one with the large lace collar. She added the diamond earrings her parents gave her when she graduated from the University of Texas with a music degree.

It was time for her husband Isaiah's funeral. She frowned into the mirror, doing her best to look the bereaved widow, but in her heart she felt like singing the "Hallelujah Chorus", really loud.

Mabel created a private world of music in her mind long ago. She taught herself to begin each day humming a happy tune. Three mornings before, she rolled out of bed as usual, hummed her song, and prepared breakfast.

"Isaiah!" she called. "It's Sunday! Hurry up." When he didn't appear dressed for preaching, she went to their bedroom door and realized he hadn't moved. In fact, he wasn't breathing. He was as dead as the sermon notes on his bedside table.

Isaiah had always been a miserable man, only happy when he could make her as miserable as he was. She should never have married him sixteen years earlier but when he took an interest in her she was twenty-six, an old maid with no marriage prospects. She only had one love in her life and it was an impossible situation.

Mabel was the organist at her neighborhood church, and Isaiah, the new junior minister was full of himself and full of God. Through the years she realized Isaiah used God as a source of power and control, but he didn't serve God. She never saw him do anything charitable unless it fed his oversized ego.

Nonetheless, she had married him and once a lady married she was to stay that way, especially if she chose to marry a preacher. Mabel survived with her music and by corresponding with her good friend. No matter what, Isaiah couldn't do a thing about that.

Preacher Pevey never progressed to churches bigger than 150 members. It seemed once a congregation added that one hundred and fifty-first member the crowd was fed up with his self-serving attitude and lack of interesting sermons. They would find a way to have God call him onward to another small community. Mabel followed, playing the organ and leading the choirs. She spent hours a day playing the large Steinway grand piano her parents gave her, insisting it follow them wherever they lived.

When Isaiah was called to serve the El Chico Methodist Church the previous year, they bought a small frame house near the high school. Mabel crowded the piano into the tiny living room, leaving space for several small chairs and a cabinet full of sheet music. A large oak tree shaded three large windows enclosing the piano room and the small entryway porch. She planted some flowers in the adjoining rock-lined beds, giving her more pleasure than she'd had in decades.

El Chico citizens loved a good funeral. The Methodist Church was packed with overheated citizens, standing room only, when Mabel arrived. She recognized Marjorie Plunker, Ethel Ogletree, Etta Ruth Foremost, and Bea McPherson sitting in their usual pew. They waved and she tried hard to look sad. Lester Plunker, the lead Deacon, beadlets of sweat pouring from his plastered-down hair, gave the tribute. It was as boring and self-serving as Isaiah, making Carly Simon's tune, "You're So Vain" run through Mabel's mind. In the church's multi-purpose hall the ladies provided fruit punch and home-baked cookies. One by one people stood in line to share their condolences. Mabel knew most felt the same way she did, glad to be free of the man.

Bea McPherson came up behind the new widow and whispered in her ear, "No one else is gonna say this to you, but I will 'cause I see the truth in your eyes. Your husband's death, while sad for him, is a blessing for you. You'll miss him, I know. But, remember, girl, if you lived with a rattlesnake for sixteen years and it died, you'd miss it, too. The church ladies and I want you to know we hope you'll stay in El Chico." Bea gave Mabel a big hug. "If you ever need to talk, you know where I am."

"Thanks, Bea. You are the one woman in town I can call 'friend.'"

"One, two, toss. One, two, throw." That night Mabel hummed The Blue Danube Waltz as she emptied Isaiah's closet into large trash bags. She put his never-used tools, his stack of religious magazines and every last possession, including his Jesus coffee mug, into boxes and placed them on her front porch. Early the next morning she hauled the stuff to a nearby thrift shop singing, "I'm Gonna Wash that Man Right Out of My Hair" at the top of her voice.

Then Mabel swept, mopped, and scrubbed every corner of her little house. She dressed in her favorite flowered dress, let down her bun and combed her hair down her back, powdered some blush across her cheeks, put on some red lipstick, sat down at the Steinway and played for three hours straight. The magnificent compositions by Chopin, Schubert, and Mozart wafted throughout El Chico. Her neighbors stopped talking among themselves, shut off *The Lawrence Welk Show*, and sat back to enjoy music like they'd never heard before.

A month later Mabel drove to the county seat and waited for the Greyhound to pull into the little station. Her heart swelled as she sang, "Always and forever, each moment with you, is just like a dream to me / that somehow came true."

They embraced like all lovers do when reuniting, unashamed, laughing, hugging and walking hand in hand to the car, unaware of the rest of the world. On the way to El Chico, over the rolling plains covered with mesquite and scrub oak, Mabel pointed out what was left of the cattle herds. She explained the consequences of the drought to her lifelong friend and lover. When the mountain appeared she stopped the car at the side of the highway to show the striking beauty of the landmark.

Reaching out for her sweetheart's hand, Geraldine spoke softly, "So, there it is, exactly like you told me in all your letters. I love it already, just like you do."

"Yes, I think we'll be happy in El Chico. Of course we'll have to be 'just friends' to the public, but we're used to that," said Mabel, gazing into Geraldine's eyes.

The two women savored each room as they toured the little white house, especially the one holding the Steinway, a variety of other instruments and shelves of music. The room was ready with flowers, a bottle of cooled champagne and a shiny new brass music stand. Geraldine removed her violin from its case. Mabel sat at the piano and the two played "Moonlight Sonata" together.

The next Monday morning Chester Cartwright erected a sign in Mabel's front yard. It was painted white, with crisp black letters, "Piano and Violin Lessons – Instructors: Mabel Pevey and Geraldine Whitfield – Open for Business."

SWEET CHARITY

"It's a sad, sad fact. Juanita Gutierrez has got the cancer," said Lulu Belle Schwartz, curling iron waving in the air. The ladies were quieter than usual, depressed about the recent news. "I stopped by her place to cheer her up, fixed her hair and gave her a healin candle. It's one of them new air-roma-therapy ones, lemon and lavender."

It was Friday and most of the women in the beauty group were assembled at the Cut 'n Curl. Whether they were having a hair or nail treatment, or nothing at all, no one dared miss Friday's gossip fest for fear of being the subject of the day.

"Hi ever-body!" Odelia said, swinging the front door open, bells jingling, alerting the group that someone new had arrived. She placed a large cardboard box on a small table usually reserved for nail polishes and face creams. "I brought a special treat today all the way from Sam's Club. It's cinnamon coffee and French pastries. I was over at the county seat yesterday and thought to myself, 'why not celebrate just being alive?' " She looked around at the sad faces. "What's the matter? You'll love these goodies. Now is a time for us to give ourselves a boost in light of Preacher Pevey's passing and Juanita's health condition."

"What do you think of this new *Plum Pink* nail color?" Asked Etta Ruth. She flashed her nails at the covey of women dressed in pink curlers and nylon kimonos looking like very large cupcakes lined up in a bakery case.

"How can you talk about nail color at a time like this?" criticized Lulu. "What will happen to the twins if Juanita cain't get well? I know you girls have been critical of her, but if you knew what she puts up with, well, you'd be more understandin. It seems to me, havin a no-good husband like she does is enough for anybody to deal with in this life."

Bea glanced around the room as she paid for a bottle of Lulu's special shampoo and conditioner. "Frankly, ladies, I'm happy to see this group's concern for someone who used to be the subject of very negative gossip."

Minnie Lee spoke up, pulling her head out of the dryer, shutting it off to hear what all the talking was about. "Well, Bea, you should know we've had two prayer vigils at the church for her and plan for another Wednesday evening. Joe Ray was there and I think he has stopped drinkin. Handing the problem over to Jesus; trustin Him to heal is the answer."

"How many times do I have to remind you that his name is Jose`, not Joe Ray? You'd think you'd remember by now." Lulu frowned and waved her pointing finger back and forth at the group in rebuke.

"Well, we called him Joe Ray at the prayer vigils. I hope the good Lord got the message and knew who we were talkin about." Minnie Lee pulled curlers out of her hair.

"Praying and then goin about your business as usual is always your solution," said Bea. "I'm not saying real uplifting praying doesn't help, but I will point out that cancer keeps killin people in spite of thousands of prayers going up each day. This is a time for action."

Etta Ruth, still sorting through nail polishes, stopped to add, "I have to agree with Bea. Another prayer vigil is good, Minnie Lee, but we need somethin else. Poor little Juanita needs chemo drugs and she cain't afford them. They have not had in-surance ever since Joe Ray, I mean Jose`, was laid off from that landscaping company."

"Well then, Etta Ruth, why don't you dip into your stash and fork over a few dollars to start a fund?" said Odelia.

"I don't know why it always has to be me that gives money. Surely someone else in this town has some stuffed in a boot or under a rock. Just maybe all the Gutierrez family should take care of their own," said the Mayor's wife as she spun around in a pink Naugahyde chair. She checked the gray roots showing though her died black locks.

"Etta Ruth, we all know they are the only Mexican family in Texas without any relatives. Poor little Juanita was left an orphan when she was twelve. She needs help from us." Odelia glared at her friend. "I took a tuna casserole over to Juanita's last night. My Auntie swore by its healin powers. There she was with those two precious children and Jose`ph Ray sittin on the couch watching bullfight reruns. It was the saddest sight I've seen in a long time."

As she applied a glob of black color to Etta Ruth's hair, Lulu responded, "I just 'bout cry my eyes out when I see her body waistin away like it is."

Suddenly, Marjorie Plunker, white lace slip fluttering under the floral kimona, ran to the shop's door and swung it open. "Oh my Gosh! Did you see that? It was him! I saw the chief again." She looked down the long sidewalk trying to get a look at the mysterious man and his long black braids. He was not there.

Lulu Belle followed Marjorie, looking right and then left, attempting to see the Native American. "I think I saw a flash of silver, but it's gone now."

Taking another huge bite of her sweet roll, Minnie Lee mumbled, "You girls are always sayin you saw him but I never have, 'cept for the night at the town meeting when he volunteered to do some kind of weird ceremony to bring water back to El Chico. I think these sightings are all in your imaginations."

"Jake has known Silver Crow most all his life and tells me the man is powerful, can make unimaginable things happen," said Bea in a firm voice. "He says the Chief appears from nowhere, like smoke, when Jake's out checking the cattle and that's miles out in the wilderness. So, I'm saying, it's probably true that he was just walking around El Chico and you got a glimpse. Honestly, ladies, I think you need to give some serious thought to taking him up on his proposition. Native American ceremonies were used for centuries to help The People though droughts. I don't see how it could possibly hurt."

CATS AND CACTUS

Ed and Odelia Hawkins, gave up on dogs once their sixteen-year old Henry died. Instead, they kept eight or so almost-wild cats running around the salvage yard. They helped keep the rats and rattlers at bay. Sarah was the queen of the pack, their favorite. Most days the sleek black feline sat on the front porch watching, observing. Her sharp eyes missed little as she scanned the dried-up golf course and piles of surplus Ed accumulated. She stretched and yawned, seemed to be bored with the sweltering west Texas day. She displayed an air of superiority.

Odelia sighed, perspiration soaking her blouse. "Oh damn it to hell. Just look at this mess. Every year I had the prettiest bed of flowers in the county and now I cain't seem to get one lousy petunia to grow!" She continued to dig, uprooting the sun-fried wads of leaves and stems that used to be plants, tossing them into a basket.

Ed set a large box of cactus down at the edge of the stoned-in area that formerly was his wife's showplace. "Odelia, I ain't heard you swear in a long time. You heard what the Mayor said at the meetin. We must save what little water is left for essentialities like drinkin."

"I know cursin is not a ladylike thing to do but the ground is as hard as cement and these cactus are about as appealing as goat poop."

"Butro Gibbons, the new County Extension Agent, said cactus are friendly to the environment and cactus flowers will sprout all summer long providing an abundance of enjoyment." Ed watched Odelia as she dug in the rock-hard soil. For the first time in his life he thought of closing his business and moving away from El Chico.

"Hi there, y'all." Mary Nelle and Marjorie crunched up the long gravel driveway that circled around the office and ended at the small frame house. They leaned out the windows of the faded green Oldsmobile 88. The wraparound chrome bumpers reflected the sun into Odelia's and Ed's eyes causing them to squint and shade their faces with their hands like a salute. Sarah turned over, returning to her sunbathing.

"Aren't you goin to the Church Circle this afternoon?" shrieked Marjorie over the sound of the car's motor.

"No, cain't go today. We're redoing the flower bed with these boulders off the mountain and cactus plants Ed got over at Cattle Country Nursery," said Odelia walking over to greet her friends.

Ed grabbed the opportunity for a break. He walked back into the house, poured a glass of iced tea and sat down to get a glimpse of *Days of Our Lives*. Ed wouldn't admit it, but he was addicted to the soap opera and the garden project was getting in the way of his program schedule.

The ladies exchanged a few more words and the visitors backed out and disappeared into the heat waves bouncing off the highway.

Odelia returned to her digging and pulling as Sarah made her way slowly down the porch steps rubbing against the boulders and examining the new cactus. Around and around she went, her nose in the air in disapproval. Using as little energy as possible, she continued her elegant walk, climbing back to the porch. She stretched, rolled over, flapped her tail, cleaned her paws and fur, then returned to her previous observation post. Odelia, covered with sweat and dirt, turned to Sarah and frowned.

Ed came out the door, refreshed from his TV break. He took one look at the scene. "On TV they say we need to learn one new word each day and the new word for the day is 'nonchallenge.' Cats are examples of nonchallenge. It means indifferent, like they don't give a damn."

Odelia glared at her husband. "Hellfire! Then, Ed, that makes you the King of Nonchalance, not 'nonchallenge.' I hate to start a fight, but lately you seem plain lazy and like you don't care about anything. All you do is watch TV, hit golf balls around the property and meet with that town council that does nothing about El Chico's problems."

Seeing Odelia's eyes filled with scorn and disappointment was like having a dagger plunged into his heart. That's all it took for Ed to know just how much he cared about his wife, his town, and their lives in El Chico. He vowed to himself to do everything he could to make Odelia happy and to see that the town survived. Tomorrow he would start his search for a secondhand water tower.

PERCY

"Percy, Percy! Wake up!" Etta Ruth shook her husband. He awakened her before dawn from a deep sleep with his screaming and moaning. He was soaked in sweat, head twitching and body shaking all over like he was having a seisure.

"Oh God! Oh God!" said the El Chico mayor. "I'm fallin into the pit."

"You're just having a dream, a nightmare. Again." said his wife rubbing his back.

"It's that dream, Etta Ruth, the one I keep havin about the mountain swallowing me up whole. It was awful, like being crushed by a monster."

"Sweetie Pie, it must have been the refried beans you ate, or the chimichanga, or the chocolate-peanut-butter ice cream," consoled his wife. "Let's get up and have some Tums, some coffee, and a bowl of Wheaties. I'm sure that'll make you feel better."

The mayor had been dreaming the same dream for two months almost every night and was weary from the loss of sleep. In the dream, he and Graystone were throwing money in the air at the top of the mountain where acres of a beautiful resort surrounded them. Then Janelle appeared, the ground shook and he fell into a bottomless pit, surrounded by swirling rings of fire amidst the darkest dark he had ever seen.

After breakfast he felt better and was ready to drive the two blocks to the City Hall meeting room. It was Wednesday and he was not looking forward to another session with the council discussing the pipeline, water tower, or the Indian's alternative solution to the drought. The past few meetings had ended in near fistfights, and nothing resolved.

"Will the meetin come to order," Percy slammed his gavel on the table. "Can we dispense with the minutes? They'll be the same as last week and the week before that."

"I move we don't have Bea read the minutes," said Herb Matson as he poured himself a cup of coffee and grabbed a doughnut. "Anyone else want a doughnut? Fresh from Walmart?"

The men looked at each other and scooted their chairs close around the T-formation. They passed doughnuts and coffee along the line, ending with the mayor who was sitting at the head of the tables. He began the discussion. "Men, I think we need to go over the ideas we have for gettin water once again. The pipeline seems like the eventual solution but right now we just don't have the money for the entire project. However, I propose we give H_2O Engineering a down payment now to hold them and then begin to formulate a tax plan to raise the rest."

Oliver Brumfeld straightened his bowtie and stood like a private at attention. He talked an octave higher than his usual screechy voice, causing everyone in the room to clinch their jaws. "Last meeting I thought we all agreed we'd start with a pre-owned water tower, get the town's interest and then try for raising funds for the pipeline. What happened to that?"

Like every week, Bea sat in a corner and took the minutes detailing the meeting and writing something newsworthy for the *El Chico Times Gazette*. She bit her lip, scowled, and thought, *Button it up and just do your job. Surely they'll have common sense enough to stop the insanity that seems to be driving this ridiculous pipeline idea.*

Doug Farnsworth, who never raised his voice, almost shouted. "If we're voting, I'm voting 'no' on raising taxes for the pipeline. The project needs more study."

"I'm with Doug on this. We simply do not have the funds for a pipeline," Herb Matson, the accountant in the group, was always aware of the bottom line.

Ed stood up, red-faced with anger. "But we have to do something about the water pressure. Somehow we've got to get a tower and pumpin system goin. We can do this if I can find us a tower."

"The future. Think of the future! The aquifer is running out and we have to have water to fill the tower." Wilmur White joined the men who were standing. "I'm with Percy. We have to get the pipeline."

The argument went on ending with Oliver, Lester, and Wilmur siding with the pipeline idea and Ed, Doug and Herb objecting.

"Will everyone please sit down?" Percy slammed his gavel. "I am ending the discussion this way. Since it's a tied situation, I get to decide. Ed will search for the tower and bring figures to our next meeting. Meanwhile, we'll send a deposit to H_2O Engineering as an expression of El Chico's eventual commitment to the pipeline project."

Bea was the only silent one in the room. She was so furious she was afraid to speak. Something had to be done to get the rest of the town to see that they were investing funds with little hope of getting water. Bea wrote hard and fast knowing when her next article appeared in the *El Chico Times Gazette* the town would be in an uproar. Sending Nicholas Graystone and his company a check would insure El Chico's coffers were going, and going fast.

OLD FRIENDS

The rising sun peaked over the eastern horizon, casting an orange glow throughout the prairie's sloping terrain. It was already hot enough to produce a sweat that evaporated as soon as it appeared, leaving a salt residue around Jake's well-worn Stetson. He guided Pearce through the rocks and thorny bushes lining the trail up the mountain looking for pipeline company markers.

He made his way through groves of scrub oaks. About half the gnarled trees were as gray and lifeless as rocks. He swung his long legs over the saddle and scrambled down a small path left by deer, back when the area was crowded with them. The count from the Texas Wildlife Board showed more than a quarter of the deer population was gone, starved. All kinds of animal carcasses dotted the Circle McP providing a bounty for scavengers.

Jake's crooked smile showed affection as he greeted the muscular man who appeared a few yards away.

Silver Crow nodded. He held an oak branch in his graceful hands. Both men knelt down and examined the dried wood. "It's very bad. The worse I've ever seen. My grandfather told me if the scrub oaks die the land won't come back for generations."

Both men continued walking, scrutinizing the terrain, shaking heads and sharing samples here and there. The native pointed to a rock formation. "Here's where the main spring surfaced. The land is angry after years of being treated with disrespect, used and abused like a whore."

Jake frowned, "Did your grandfather have any ideas for bringin the water back or getting the rain to come our way?"

"What's occurring now is new. I don't think my ancestors could have imagined the rate civilization would deplete mother earth. Back then The People revered the earth. There was never waste. Everything was recycled as a way of life. There were no petrochemicals circulating in the air. What can we do in a world like this?"

Silver Crow and Jake walked in silence until they crested the summit of the sawed-off mountain. What was once an oasis was now a ragged crater left by the silica miners when the business closed in the 60s.

"There's nothing here, no wild grass, no budding mesquite, not even cactus. The earth is sending us a message loud and clear: 'I am dying.' In a few short years this will be El Chico. Rock, nothing but rock, and maybe some dust. Consider that only a few generations back the grasses were waist deep from here to the Dakotas with bison herds in the millions."

The two friends climbed down to a secluded grove of trees hiding a circle of boulders. Together they sat on the smooth, sparkling silicon-filled pillars arranged hundreds of years ago by ancient people. "Here is the holy place." Silver Crow climbed to the top of the highest stone and with his eyes closed stood facing east. "*Ya ta say ni'. Pila mita.*" His chant began softly, "*He-ay-hee-ee. Haho. Oo-oohey. Wakan wakin tu. Ku. He-ay-hee-ee.*" (Greetings earth. My thanks. I call the Great Spirit. Look at this. It is time thunder and water come back. I call the Great Spirit.) Crow's voice soared like a vapor after a rainstorm.

Jake began the dance he learned from Silver Crow when they were teenagers. He turned and twisted, feet rising off the ground as if propelled by the air itself. His arms went above his head and then back to his sides like an eagle preparing to fly. Both men flowed to another dimension, another time, as they moved their bodies around and around. The chant of the ancient people continued. "*He-ay-hee-ee*" filtered across the sacred mountain, into the sky and downward into the abyss where The People once worshipped when it was a sparkling peak.

THE TOWER

"Gentlemen and lady, the meeting will convene. I believe we all know how important it is for us to take action. Due to the recent article appearing in the *Times Gazette*, there are those who doubt our decisions. Ms. McPherson, I am sure you will report favorably in your article *this* week, won't you?" The mayor glared at Bea.

Bea sat in the corner taking notes. She smiled and nodded. "I always try to report *accurately*, Mr. Mayor."

"I don't think discussing the feasibility of building a tower deserves more time," said Lester Plunker wearing his customary J.C. Penney's business suit, hair slicked down with Brylcreem. He held up a copy of the city's bank statement. "We aren't going bankrupt. At least not yet."

"Yes, you're right, Lester. We seem to be holding our own, budget-wise, and we did pretty much agree to buying a used tower," said the mayor.

Herb Matson passed around a list of figures. "I worked up a complete report on my brand new Apple computer showing the results of Ed's search.

New computer. That's important news, thought Bea as she looked over Herb's data.

"This report is downright pretty. Congratulations on taking us into the new age. These high tech computers are a bit scary to most of us," said Wilmur White, who still used a 1950s cash register and hand-written ledger at his store.

"The numbers add up as usual, Herb. You're the best accountant in town," added Doug.

"He's the only accountant in town," said Ed Hawkins, making

everyone laugh.

Turning to Ed, Doug Farnsworth stopped the joking. "What have you found out about a used tower?"

After checking each member's eyes to be sure they were paying proper attention, Ed leaned in as if he was sharing a national security secret. Then he spoke with enthusiasm. "After some hard lookin around, I found a beauty over in Abilene. She's rusty and needs lots of work, but has all the fittings and even four of the five legs that hold a big round globe. That's fine because she'll be leaning against the mountain anyway. It would take a third of our budget to buy it but that's only a fraction of a new one. The amount on the report Herb made on his computer includes renting a large flatbed to haul her over here."

Herb smiled. "I think you will see clearly what we have budgeted for this calendar year and what the expected tax income will be for the rest of the year. We can swing buying the tower, but affording the installation is another matter."

"I'm sure we can get all the town muscle to help and somehow we'll make this happen," said Doug

The mayor smiled, "I know you fellows will pitch in, the sheriff and coach will, and if Henry Logan'll stay off the sauce, he can join the team, too. Gentlemen, if we approve this today at least we're goin forward."

Ed rubbed his hands together, anxious to start the project. "We can unload 'er at the base of the mountain over behind the motel, right in the gap where the main spring used to surface."

"Why do we have to do this at the gap? That's the creepiest place in town," The mayor frowned and broke out in a sweat remembering his dreams.

"That's where the main spring comes up to the current rusted-out tank. It's where the tower has to be, plus it will be situated right for the pipeline and ASR, if that ever happens," said Doug.

"He's right. The tower has to be at the base of the mountain." Ed smiled, sensing success on a tower acquisition.

"Great, men. Then it's decided. Ed will purchase the Abilene tower and get it moved over here," said the mayor. "And we'll send H2O a check as deposit on their future services." In all the excitement the council agreed to the mayor's proposal. He was happier by the minute thinking of Graystone's reaction when he learned the town was funding the tower and sending his retainer. Their secret corporation's next step would be to secure more land for The Etta Hotel, Resort, and Country Club.

There was laughing, handshaking, doughnut eating, and coffee drinking as the town fathers congratulated themselves on taking positive action.

"I want to propose one more thing," said Ed, using his most persuasive sales voice. "I move that the town make the Founder's Day Parade and Celebration into the biggest we've ever had so we can raise the funds needed to repair the tower and paint it all proper. With increased ticket sales, booth rentals, bazaar sales, and food revenues we can make this happen."

All the men voted to approve his proposal.

Ed, excited with the camaraderie, patted the backs of his co-council members.

Oliver Brumfield raised his voice to get the group's attention. "How about the high school art department volunteering to build a fiberglass Horn Toad to place on top of the tower?"

"Great idea, Oliver, but they, like all of us, will need money for supplies." Ed continued, "If it's okay, Bea, you could head publicity and invite all the neighboring towns to Founder's Day. Odelia says she'll head the arts and crafts committee."

The next week Ed made the final deal for the tower and Graystone opened the official City of El Chico envelope. The man from Dallas grinned. "Ha, ha. Now we're cookin." He made out a deposit slip for the special slush fund account that allowed him his lavish lifestyle.

BE LOVELY BOUTIQUE

Temperatures and tempers were blazing all over West Texas. For two weeks the daytime thermometer had not registered any number under ninety-eight and had hit 116 three times.

News headlines in Dallas, Midland, and Lubbock didn't feature the governor threatening to withdraw Texas from the United States or the Cowboys' hiring a new defensive coach. Instead, each newspaper and TV channel showed the familiar shape of the state covered with high temperatures in bright red. Young weather women with low cut blouses, big boobs, and long coiffured hair issued warnings to seniors and small children. "Stay inside your homes. Drink lots of icewater."

Clusters of gray and white clouds flew past El Chico as teasers, reminders of past rainy days when pastures of green grass and reservoirs of cool water fed the area's cattle.

"I'm tellin you it's the dyin truth," said Marjorie, her long gray braid piled high on her head to keep it off her sweating neck. She spoke to the group of women gathering outside the Be Lovely Boutique. "My brother over in Abilene says if we don't start getting steady rain soon the aquifer will be totally dry, there won't be a sheep or chicken left alive, and we'll all be forced to move to Houston or some awful place like that."

"There's nothin like a Texas heat wave," replied Odelia, perspiration running between her breasts as she flapped her arms in the air to create a breeze. "I have never been so hot in all my life. We could fry eggs on an Armadillo's back."

"The heat is makin folks behave like they're already in hell." A disheveled Bea, frizzy red curls tied in a pony tail, freckles more pronounced than usual, fanned herself with a copy of the *El Chico Times Gazette* as she made a mini-report to the gathering.

"First of all, Juanita is not doing any better fighting the cancer. She cain't afford the treatments so please support the fund raising for her every time you can. Secondly, the City Council met again yesterday. Thanks to Ed's skill at finding bargains, we are buying a used tower to replace our rusted tank. We need money for the installation so we'll use Founders Day as our fundraiser. That means we all have to work together to make it the biggest and best yet. And next, a down payment was sent to H_2O Engineering. Some council members were afraid to try the free Native American rain ceremony but weren't afraid to empty the treasury for a down payment on an untested pipeline idea."

"Well, Bea, I for one am a believer in Nicholas Graystone's work and can't understand why you have any doubts. I think the town would be well served to have him as the Founder's Day celebrity, ex-Cowboy football star and all. My husband, the mayor, says so." Etta Ruth reminded everyone of her special status in the community.

"Joe Farnsworth, our local hero, is our favorite. He could bring some of Lyle's boys with him and add a real flare to the celebration." Odelia winked at Bea to let her know she and Ed were on her side.

"You ladies just don't know how stressed Percy is over all his responsibilities. He's havin nightmares, even wakin up screamin. Everyone in town is complaining to him about the new conservation rules not wantin to limit their showers or flushes." Etta Ruth rummaged through a box of necklaces and earrings. "Do y'all think these dangles look good on me?"

"Well, since you asked, they are entirely too large for your face." Bea frowned.

Odelia leaned over to get a closer look. "Etta Ruth, bless your heart, I have to agree with Bea." The women's shopping resumed.

Bea, tried to reason with the woman, but did a slow burn inside. "Etta Ruth, I do hope you and Percy will reconsider and not invite that Graystone fella to be our honoree. Granted he is handsome and has a personality like a movie star, but none of us really knows him and we all know Joe Farnsworth."

"Needless to say, I hope Joe is the honoree along with our dog, Ten-Four," said Wilma Farnsworth as she held a bright orange tee shirt next to her torso. "But, Etta Ruth, honey, Doug and I'll support whoever is selected, no hard feelins."

The women chitchatted discussing the recent news as they looked through merchandise. Two times a year Lulu Belle Swartz, owner of the Be Lovely Boutique, lined racks, tables and shelves outside her store. She stuffed them with every item she had in stock and then stretched a big sign across the establishment's windows that said, *"MAKE ME AN OFFER".*

Folding chairs and card tables were spread out along the narrow walking space. Dolly Nelson stood behind a display of sandwiches and cold drinks. No one was buying the sandwiches but the cold drinks were almost sold out and it wasn't even noon. Dolly filled plastic bags with crushed ice and offered them for a dollar each. "Just slip these little ditties inside your bras and you can keep on shopping in comfort." The women lined up for her bra coolers.

Lulu Belle's sales were legendary. Crowds of ladies showed up from miles around expecting bargains and camaraderie. Today they were screaming across each other, bidding on the blouses, jeans, purses, and jewelry. Like the floor of the New York Stock Exchange, it was a circus. Anyone visiting for the first time was amazed that Lulu Belle could decipher the offers through the clamor of high-pitched female voices that sounded like geese in mating season.

The frenzy continued in spite of the heat. Sweating women, arms heaped high with garments, sorted through the colorful stacks and racks.

"That little turquize shirt, or one almost like it, was featured in the Neiman Marcus catalogue last year," yelled Lulu to Etta Ruth, knowing the woman could never resist anything that might convince her friends it was from Neiman's.

"I'll take it! I'll take it!" Etta Ruth shouted back. She had no idea what size the shirt was or if it would go with anything she owned but no own else in town would get it.

"I saw it first," said an exotic, olive skinned woman with wide horn-rimed glasses outlining her large, chocolate colored eyes. She waved the garment high in the air. "It's my size, way too small for you." She flipped her long, raven hair across her shoulders, held on to the bright cloth and resumed shopping.

"And who does she think she is?" Etta Ruth said to Bea as she looked daggers at the stranger. She turned and scooted down the sidewalk closer to her adversary. "That shirt's mine!" she shrieked.

Bea squinted to put the unknown female into focus. She had never seen her before but it was clear this person was not familiar with Etta Ruth's wrath when she didn't get her way. Since Percy had become mayor, Etta Ruth Foremost crowned herself queen of El Chico and every woman in town knew to avoid conflicts with her.

Etta Ruth grabbed the shirt out of the tall lady's hands. Bea saw the woman's eyes sharpen into slits, and knew the mayor's dumpy wife had met her match.

"Oh no you don't," said the stranger as she snatched the garment back.

Quicker than a slamming door, a large orange purse hit the taller woman in the head.

"**Oh shit**," said Bea, running to the conflict. It was hard to tell who was doing what. The turquoise fabric made a loud ripping sound. Another handbag swung through the air. Blouses and jeans flew like giant birds. It was all arms, hair and screeches. Clothing, jewelry, and bra coolers went everywhere as the other women joined in the uprising.

Lulu Belle and Dolly scrunched down holding on to each other. Bea climbed on top of a table gazing at the pieces of turquoise fabric scattered along the sidewalk. She did her famous only-boys-can-do-it whistle and cupped her hands in megaphone style. "SHUT UP! QUI-ET! LADIES, LADIES, FREE I-ICE TEA FOR EVERYONE! FREE I-ICE COLD TEA FOR EVERYONE."

Slowly the noise subsided and the shoppers located their purses and dignity. Bea got down from her perch and leaned over to help Lulu Belle and Dolly up from their foxhole positions. "Lulu Belle, go inside and brew some tea. And, Dolly, run across the street to On the Road Again and get Billy to bring a giant bucket of ice over. With lemons. And fast!"

Returning to her table podium Bea announced, "Ladies, let's not let our tempers compete with the heat. Ice tea with lemons and lots of sugar will be served as soon as we help Lulu Belle fix up this mess." She noticed the beautiful dark lady gracefully walking away, getting into a car with a handsome black man and two teenaged children.

When Bea guided her Escalade into the carport at her ranch, Jake was leaning against the ancient cottonwood near the main house. He waved and his usual near-smile crossed his face at the sight of her. He opened the car door and walked beside her until they both collapsed into porch rocking chairs.

Placing his hat on the weathered railing, Jake frowned. "Hate to greet you with bad news, but you should know. The front well is almost dry. I'm real worried for Duke Five. He needs about twenty-five gallons of water a day in this heat and he's almost drinkin mud."

Rocking back and forth letting the breeze cool her as Jake's words sank in, Bea looked at the man who was always there for her. "Sounds like we have some serious stuff to talk about, Jake. Just wait 'til I tell you what else happened because of this heat wave." She frowned and rocked. "We just had an all-lady riot at the Be Lovely Boutique. Downtown El Chico came close to being another Alamo."

"Oh God! Why don't you tell me all about it over a glass of lemonade, but, it seems we'll need to add a dose of tequila on the side."

THE MEN

The council spent the entire two-hour meeting arguing about who the Founder's Day Parade honoree would be. Once again the mayor broke the tie vote deciding Nicholas Graystone was the choice.

"Damn it to hell!" Bea exclaimed under her breath.

"I take it you're not happy with this decision, Miss McPherson." said the mayor, not hiding his hostility.

"You can say that again." Bea stalked out of the meeting.

The next day Ed Hawkins and his group of merry men made their way to Abilene's city dump where the dilapidated remains of a water tower were stored. Ed drove the rented flatbed with Chester Cartwright and Henry Logan as sidekicks. Next were Lester, Wilmur, and the coach in the White's family minivan. At the tail end of the procession Doug Farnsworth and the sheriff followed in the El Chico police car.

The city of Abilene was so glad to be rid of the mass of rusty steel that they furnished the crane needed to lift the large pieces of metal and manpower to secure it to the gigantic truck. Abilene even agreed to transport their crane to El Chico to help with unloading.

"Now men, these here red flags must be secured at each point on our load so we don't obscure vision for all vehicles utilizing Lonestar highways. I'm adhering to the code and laws of Texas that apply when transporting oversized objects," said the sheriff, taking charge as he attached the flags to the huge globe, the truck and the crane.

It took them more than five hours to get the sixty miles back to

El Chico. Anyone passing them on the road might think a small planet had fallen from the sky onto the back of the oversized trailer. The parade of vehicles entered the El Chico city limits and circled around the backside of the Ranger Motel with the sheriff's lights blazing. They parked at the base of the mountain where the current water pumping system was ready for the new tower.

A group of well-wishers was waiting, cheering the arrival of the unusual addition to the town. Wilma Farnsworth and others had packed huge coolers with enough food to feed the small army.

Etta Ruth forced the Mayor to be there. "You cain't be tellin the council to support the pipeline if you don't show up to the tower arrival."

"You don't understand. This place gives me the willies. It's just like in my dream. What if it opens up and swallows me? I'm tellin you the Indians spooked this whole mountain. I think they put a hex on it with all their native prayers and such. And then, to boot, the tower looks like a spaceship. All we need is for Ed and his friends to dress up in alien costumes. They'd scare anyone to death."

Bea and Jake were standing in the crowd. "I wonder if this damned old tower will be of any use at all? It looks pretty bad."

"Well, if having the tower raises the town's spirits, it'll be worth it," Jake smiled, happy to be next to Bea. "Come on. It won't hurt to be a little happy about this." He hugged her. Then cheered along with a nearby group of high school athletes.

"I hope you're right and that it's not the beginning of the end," said Bea, surprised and glad about Jake's sudden show of affection.

☆ ☆ ☆

Unknown to the gathering, Silver Crow stood observing, arms crossed at his chest, on a ledge near the top of the mountain. With bowed head, he raised his hands and looked skyward. "He-ay-hee-ee. Haho. Oo-oohey." He chanted in the ancient language, asking for this treasured piece of earth to be restored.

PROGRESS

For the next few weeks at the Friday beauty meeting, conversations centered on Juanita Gutierrez's cancer, her rapid decline, the plight of her kids and the lack of funds for treatments. This resulted in both Baptists and Methodists holding separate prayer vigils, then joining forces with the City Council to produce a big Spaghetti Dinner Fundraiser to pay for chemotherapy. A large anonymous donation was received and the doctors began treatments.

That same week an unidentified donor had two new Mac computers installed at the library, plus four at the high school, replacing outdated equipment. An expert was also scheduled to drive over from the county seat four days a week to teach computer classes to anyone who signed up.

The ladies were in a dither, each one talking louder than the one next to her.

"Ed starts his computer lessons tomorrow so I'm joinin him." Odelia was excited about her news. "We're learning how to use the Internet. Ed wants to have a website for his business."

"Well, we wish you luck with all the new techno stuff. It's over my head." Ethel thumbed through the latest copy of *People* magazine and then looked at Etta Ruth and winked. "I just wonder who donated those computers and if it was the same person that gave so much to the Juanita Fund."

"Now listen, y'all. Juanita was tellin me about a vision that's healing her," said Lulu Belle.

"That poor girl is hallucinatin. It's all the drugs I've been payin for, that is, along with some of you that have also joined the Juanita Gutierrez fundraiser group," added Etta Ruth.

Mary Nelle Matson sat in the new, pink floral chair with clusters of aluminum foil holding her locks in suspension as bleach drained the mousy russet to blond. "I just knew it was you who did all that donatin. You're too sweet for words, Etta Ruth."

"I'll never tell a soul if I did or didn't," said Etta Ruth not wanting to admit she was not the donor, wondering who was.

Bea changed the subject. "So, Juanita is feelin better?"

"All I know is she said a great vision, like an angel, visits her everyday. He's standin over her, appearing in a cloud, like a ghost. She says he chants the most beautiful chant and touches her head and waves his hands. She says she falls asleep in the most peace she's felt in months, or maybe ever," continued Lulu.

"Maybe it's not just the drugs, but a real angel." Lulu checked Mary Nelle's hair color.

"I'm sure it's Silver Crow who visits Juanita. That's his way and his gift." Bea smiled, grabbed her notebook and walked out the door into another hot day.

FIRE

J ake rode Pearce as he had in their younger days, hard and fast. They raced across the western corner of the Circle McP Ranch, zigzagging to avoid dry, craggy arroyos and dehydrated bent mesquites, all victims of the severe heat and long-term drought.

"Whoa, there." He dismounted as if he was still a rodeo cowboy. Running to his rusted pickup, he hooked the horse trailer, loading Pearce fast. Sam had already jumped into the truck's cab panting from chasing horse and rider across the parched ranchland.

Dust and pebbles flew as Jake gunned the old Ford's motor taking a half-mile shortcut through pastures to Bea's ranch house. He could smell the smoke.

Honking and yelling as he drove up the dirt driveway, his brain compiled an emergency list of things needed to save the livestock.

"Hey Jake. What's wrong?" Bea walked out to greet the foreman, screen door flapping, Buster following close behind, tail wagging in anticipation of a visit with Jake and Sam.

"Can you smell it? The fire?" The man's muscular arms gathered shovels and rakes, throwing them into the truck bed.

"Oh, my God! I can see the smoke there on the horizon," said Bea squinting as she sniffed the air. "How bad is it?"

"I cain't tell but it's not good. Bea, get into town and put out a warnin. With the area as dry as the Mojave, El Chico could catch fire. As he turned the truck and trailer around, horse and dog in tow, he yelled, "I'm goin back out to round up Duke and the cows. *Your* sheep'll take care of themselves. As dumb as they are, they'll know to run." He headed for the smoke leaving a dust cloud in his wake.

Bea backed her Escalade out of the carport and headed into El Chico before Jake reached the edge of the pasture.

Within thirty minutes Sheriff Darnell was going street-to-street, siren and loudspeaker blasting announcements about the fire. Mayor Foremost called the council members and put their emergency civil defense program into action. Percy was quick to point out this program was designed under his leadership and this was the first time they'd had an opportunity to try it out.

Marjorie organized the Church Ladies Guild with Mary Nelle leading the group in prayer.

"Thank God your prayer was short. We need to get busy with our part of the plan," said Ethel, adorned in a fireman's hat and jacket her dearly departed husband left in his closet.

"All mothers and children need to assemble immediately at the high school cafeteria accordin to our Civil Defense Action Plan," said a bossy Etta Ruth. "Ladies, begin your telephone alert calls now."

Odelia, as wife of Fire Chief Ed, was first to arrive at the high school to prepare the cafeteria and gym area for refugees. "I had one of my Double Chocolate Cakes in the freezer so I brought it along," she announced to the volunteers as they arrived.

Marjorie patted Odelia on the shoulder. "I'll put the centerpieces out on the tables. They're a bit dusty from being stored in the attic but they'll help keep everyone's spirits up during the crisis."

An out-of-breath, Lulu Belle, arms loaded with boxes announced, "Here's the matchin aprons for the committee ladies. I've had them stored in the *Be Lovely Boutique's* closet along with a stack of napkins just waiting for our first disaster. And, Lordy, Lordy, here it is!"

Dolly and Billy Nelson arrived, pickup loaded with food. She shouted as they entered through the cafeteria's back door. "Here you go! We emptied On the Road Again's collection of condiments, lettuce and tomatoes. Billy's bringing in a week's worth of barbequed brisket with a gallon of his secret sauce."

Meanwhile, Fire Chief Ed Hawkins prepared to meet the firefighters, putting his part of the Civil Defense Plan into action. Brushing his mane of graying hair into a dented vintage fire helmet, Ed made his way through the salvage yard to the far corner of his property where his golf course backed up to the town's cemetery.

A thirty-year-old fire truck was parked under a large tent formerly used by a traveling circus. The tent featured faded paintings of an elephant, a ringmaster, and a trapeze artist.

Ed smiled as the antique engine, hoses folded and ladder suspended across the top, started up with only a few backfires. In minutes the motor settled down to a loud and steady rumble. The old vehicle bumped across the cemetery fence line and onto the road, hardly disturbing any of the interred, until it got to old Bert Williams in his family's plot. "Sorry Bert, it's an emergency," yelled the Fire Chief.

Ed's eyes burned from the thickening smoke as he guided the shinny red relic to the parking lot outside the high school gym. Seeing the seven volunteer firefighters at attention, all lined up like eggs in a carton made Ed proud. They had practiced the drill for over a year and this emergency would prove their strength and ability.

Oliver Brumfeld, wavy hair plastered across his forehead as usual, saluted with one hand and waved his bright red fire hat with the other. *Where in the hell did he find that get-up?* Ed thought as he scrutinized Oliver's yellow jacket, shiny black boots and red hatchet attached with a belt at his waist.

And damn it if Lester Plunker didn't come from his bank office, because he's still wearing his special J.C. Penney suit. He must wear it to bed each night. Never seen him in normal clothes. Ed's thoughts then turned to the disaster.

"Jump aboard, men! We're going to follow the smoke. Bea says Jake is waitin for us at the ranch." Ed screamed as loud as he could to be heard over the engine's clattering motor. Scrambling aboard, pushing and pulling, the middle-aged men struggled into place. Ed double clutched and off they went, the earsplitting siren alerting El Chico's dogs it was time to howl.

In the far corner of the ranch, Jake and Silver Crow rode through the thick smoke, Stetsons were pulled low on their heads and wet bandanas covered their faces. They allowed their horses to lead them back to the house trusting the animals' instincts over their own.

"That firebreak's gonna stop the worst of it," said Jake. "Even before your people lived in the area, these rock formations were a natural barrier for prairie fires."

"The buffalo created these paths when there were millions of them," said Silver Crow as they skirted the fire.

"The blaze must've started from a spark of dry lightning hittin prairie grass. Do ya think Bea's place is safe? And El Chico?" Jake looked to the Comanche chief for an answer.

"I believe so. Once the fire hits the big arroyo it won't have anywhere left to go unless it jumps fifty feet. That's unlikely."

"But, Crow, something just don't ring true about this fire."

"Yeah, lightnin fires don't behave this way. If I didn't know better I'd think it started from some kind of campfire, but that doesn't make sense either. There aren't any campers around here but me. I'll do some more looking around tomorrow."

"Oh holy shit, Crow! Hear that siren? Look over yonder. Here comes Ed drivin that ol truck loaded to the gills with the El Chico firefighters." Jake shook his head and laughed.

"Fifty gallons of water squirting through those old, worn-out hoses won't do a thing, but let's not tell 'em," added Silver Crow.

The horses and fire engine met at the pasture gate and the firefighters unloaded like Mexican jumping beans. "We're here to help. Our ladder and hoses can be engaged in minutes," said Lester, tie and jacket removed, shirtsleeves rolled up.

"I think it's burnin your western pastures," said Herb Matson. "Mary Nelle told me to do all I can to help you out, Jake."

"Well, men, we can see y'all are ready to fight the big blaze, but Silver Crow was on the scene before any of us and says the big arroyo firebreak is gonna do the trick." The cowboy removed his bandana and smoke-covered hat as he brushed back his scruffy gray-blond hair. "The air is already clearin because there's so little prairie grass left to burn."

"Well then, I guess we're too late to make a difference." Ed kicked the ground, disappointed.

"Great firefighters, your spirits are proud and brave men are still needed. There is a life in danger," said Silver Crow looking toward the barn.

Jake, pointed upward. "Maybe y'all can get that there goat off the roof. He musta got scared and climbed up top when the smoke was so thick. He's Bea's favorite and we wouldn't want to lose him."

When the tired and dusty firefighters returned to town, they were welcomed as heroes.

As Jake explained to the waiting crowd, "These seven volunteers have saved a life, even if it was a goat's."

Cheers rose from The El Chico Horn Toad football team, cheerleaders and Booster Club, who formed a welcome line leading to the school gym. Inside the building, the Lady's Guild had the emergency feast waiting. Mayor Foremost declared the day a success reading a proclamation to the gathered crowd over a bullhorn. The party faded into night with a full moon peeking out from the dwindling smoke.

Once at home, the Mayor called the private number in Dallas. "The big range fire here today was a success. Didn't burn anything but grass just like you planned. I heard three more families want to sell out. They're convinced we'll never recover from the drought. Our plan is right on track. I thought you'd want to know." He hung up knowing Graystone would get the message and be as happy as he was.

TEAMWORK

All over town people worked, readying for the Founders Day Festival. It would start with a parade and end with a dance. In between, a food fest and craft bazaar would entertain everyone.

The nine-member Horn Toad Drill Team practiced marching and baton twirling each afternoon with the meager high school band and cheerleading squad. Anyone below the age of ninety who owned a musical instrument pulled it out of storage, shined it up, and joined the rehearsals.

"I'm so excited about the bazaar," Lulu Belle chatted as she helped Bea unload a platform full of boxes.

"Odelia, look at the doilies I crocheted." Ethel Ogletree emptied a large grocery bag, piling the contents on the counter of the Cut 'n Curl. It was Friday and the ladies gathered, but instead of their usual glamour day, the group knitted hot pads, baby booties, and hats for the upcoming fundraiser. Cardboard boxes were stacked all over, making it hard to navigate the clothing racks and beauty equipment.

"Oh, mmmmm. These are just lovely and sure to go fast," said Odelia rummaging through the large mound of colorful items.

"Well, if you think that's somethin, just look at what I made." Etta Ruth lined up a selection of beaded earrings and necklaces beside the doilies.

"Why, Etta Ruth, I had no idea you're a jewelry artist." Lulu Belle held a pair of earrings up to her ears and gazed into the mirror. "When Founders Day is over maybe you could make some of these and sell them in my shop."

"This town is full of talent. Just look at these macaroni angels, calico aprons, napkins, and baby bibs the Church Lady's Guild is selling at their booth." Mary Nelle Matson counted inventory as she placed items in boxes readying them for sale. "Of course Wilma is making dozens of pies."

"Speaking of cooking. Marjorie and Wilma have spent days in their kitchens fixin jellies and jams. They'll have homemade peach, apple butter, and jalapeno." Bea listed all the bazaar items in a notebook while Lulu labeled and stacked them in order.

"All of this is sure to sell fast. I've sent news releases to every outlet from Dallas to Amarillo and the high school computer kids are doing some kind of high tech advertising on the Internet. We're sure to have the biggest turnout since the Founders Day Parade of 1982 when Lady Bird Johnson was here touting her Texas wildflower beautification program."

BILLY AND DOLLY

Billy Nelson's food was always one at the biggest attractions at the annual Founders Day Festival. He slow-cooked a pick-up truck full of meat over mesquite for three days using his special method. His barbeque sauce simmered for just as long, enhancing the taste of the secret ingredients. The spicy aroma wafted across the country enticing people to the festival from miles around.

On any day, because of its reputation, people drove out of their way to eat at the Nelson's On the Road Again Bar and Grill. The restaurant's location was marked by smoke rising from the nose of an old civil war canon that functioned as the chimney for the giant brick oven. It pointed into passing traffic, slowing travelers who feared they were looking down the barrel of a real weapon.

Billy Nelson was Willie's second cousin once removed, on his dad's side, and something of a celebrity in the El Chico area. He was known for his guitar playing and entertaining tales of travels with his cousin's band. His two long braids matched his reddish-gray beard and he always wore tattered skinny jeans topped off with a western-styled shirt.

Billy's wife, Dolly (no relation to "the" Dolly, but a lookalike nonetheless) contributed her famous iceberg lettuce salad to the feast. It was made with ranch dressing and lavishly sprinkled with fresh, locally made pepper bacon.

Fellow citizens completed the Founder's Day food concessions with homemade casseroles and desserts of all varieties.

CARS

Founders Day Parade Chairman, Ed Hawkins, went over his list of the dozen or so entrants signed up to join the Classic Automobile segment. Ed knew this was not an accurate title for this sector of the parade but it was good enough. Most participants didn't understand that just because their car was old, it didn't automatically qualify as classic.

He looked up and stretched his neck to see who was driving up his long drive, honking like crazy. He should have recognized the singsong, high-pitched sound. It was Chester Cartwright in his faded red 1970 Gremlin. Ed would have been embarrassed to drive the tin-can-of-a-car around even when it was new.

"Hey there," bellowed Chester as he leaned his head and long beard out the car window. "I come to thank you for the newest addition to my classic car, the hood ornament."

"Oh Lord!" Exclaimed Ed, scrambling up from his recliner, meeting Chester in front of his office. "What're you talkin about, classic? That's a sorry excuse for an au-to-mo-bile, so don't insult real classics by calling it one."

"If Jake can drive his tractor and Wilmur his Skylark, I can show off my Gremlin in the Classic Car section of the parade," whined Chester. "The wife is planning big on ridin with me; already told all her friends and ordered a new outfit from the Sears and Roebuck catalogue."

"Just kiddin. You're an important part of the parade," smiled Ed. "Percy's havin Lester drive his Fleetwood convertible so he and Etta Ruth can perch themselves on top of the back seat and wave. He's insistin on being first in line. Says it is 'befitting his position' as Mayor."

Showing every tooth he had, including the spaces where there should have been some, Chester grinned and pointed to the large chrome 1940s era Pontiac Indian Head attached to the Gremlin's hood. "It's a thing of beauty all right. Puts my car into another class for sure. It cain't compare to yours, but it suits me fine."

The two friends talked as they walked across the fourth, and last, hole in Ed's course to the old airplane hangar.

"I remember when you got this hangar, all in pieces," said Chester.

"Yep. I did a big acquirement when the government closed Bergstrom Air Force Base over in Austin."

Both men held their breath as Ed inserted a key and opened the large door. There it was. Ed's classic: a 1949 Mercury. It would be a high spot in the parade. The chrome bumpers were like quicksilver and the white-as-cotton paint, pristine.

Ed patted the hood as the two men walked around admiring the fender skirts and side pipes. Ed stroked the one small dent over the dummy spotlights and Blue Dot taillights. He popped the hood and the lifelong buddies gazed, starry-eyed, at the all-steel body. The Fresh Flathead engine's Offy Heads and TriPower Overdrive 3 Speed Transmission stared back.

As careful as a new mom, Chester removed a speck of sand with his handkerchief.

Without speaking, they closed the hood and swung open the Mercury's suicide doors, peering at the lavish backseat.

They slid into the front seat, eyes searching the glossy dashboard and elegant gearshift. Ed started the motor and they listened to the rhythm of the engine. Then Ed switched the key off and turned on the new addition to the vintage beauty, the CD player. They rested their heads on the leather seatbacks as Steppenwolf sang "Born to be Wild." Images of long-past drag races on dirt roads, long-haired girls in tight skirts, and car rides with laughing friends, stuffed on top of each other, filled their minds like a spring flood on dry West Texas plains.

Sometime later, the friends closed the hangar door, shook hands, patted each others' backs and strolled to Ed's office. It was only a week before they would show off their cars, classic or not.

FOUNDERS DAY PARADE

Jake waved and tipped his hat to Bea. She was across the road, clipboard in hand, helping the parade participants line up in the order Ed Hawkins arranged. She smiled at the handsome cowboy and chuckled to herself, realizing he sat on the ranch's old Massey Ferguson in his Sunday best.

"Jake driving a tractor, not ridin his horse, that is a sight," said Ed, walking up behind her.

"He'd better not see us laughing at him or we'll lose one of our entrants."

"Yep, and the 4H Clubbers sittin in the old wagon he's pullin would be mighty disappointed." Ed continued making his rounds.

"Hey there, Ed!" Etta Ruth waved and screamed her loudest to be heard over the commotion.

"Oh Lord in heaven. She outdid herself today." Ed mumbled when he saw Etta's outfit. She wore a long, white, sparkling dress and a crown on her head. He had to brace himself to keep a straight face. "Hi there, Etta. Mayor." The couple sat on the edge of the folded convertible top like celebrities in California's Rose Bowl Parade. "The Caddy looks great today, top down and all. You shined her up real pretty."

"Ed, just look how grand Nicholas Graystone looks." Etta pointed and waved to the honoree, right behind them in the parade line. "I've never seen a man dress like he does, a different suit for every day of the week."

Ignoring Etta, Ed turned and spoke to Lester. "Y'all are right here at the front of the parade, so that makes you the very important procession leaders. The parade will start in five minutes, so remember to lead the group on the route I gave you and end up exactly where you are now. My organizational plan leaves everyone plenty of parking space while they go to the festival."

The Mayor curled his mustache and straightened the long tail of his blue and silver brocade coat. "We hope this whole Founder's Day thing is worth all the effort and that we'll raise the money we need."

"Percy, it looks like everyone in the county turned out. We should get the funds to finish the tower, don't you worry."

Ed spoke to Bea when she joined him. "Percy must've got that outfit at a costume shop. Looks like somethin Rhett Butler would've wore."

"I guess he has to keep the peace at home and wear whatever the queen says," said Bea, rolling her eyes.

Ed's attention went to the next parade entrant. "Now this is nice, a classic Jaguar convertible brought in by our honoree. Damn it if his suit don't match the car. That beats all!"

Bea noticed the Dallas man was talking to a cluster of people like he was a regular member of the community. He saw Bea, turned away from the group and smiled. Swallowing her mistrust, Bea managed a return smile as Ed greeted Nicholas Graystone with a handshake. "We both want to thank you for being our Founder's Day honoree."

"It's my pleasure, Ed. Bea, great to see you again." Graystone didn't take his eyes off of her.

Bea wanted to ignore him, but her heart was beating fast and she was feeling as jittery as a teenaged girl. In spite of her efforts to dislike him, she found him very attractive and intriguing.

Ed smiled to himself as he noticed the looks passing between the big man and Bea. This is a first, he thought to himself, Bea flirting with a man other than Jake. He turned to honoree and said, "Just follow the mayor's car and we'll see you later, at the festival."

Before she could walk away with Ed, Graystone stepped in front of her. "Bea, I hoped maybe we could grab a bite of food together at the festival and that you could show me around."

"Well, it's nice to see you again, Nicholas." She stuttered. "I'm sure we'll see each other later, but I have lots to do to keep the events organized."

"Bea, first of all, please call me Nick. I know you have lots to do, but I'll find you at the festival and make sure we can visit, unless you object."

She smiled, waved and walked away, then turned around and smiled again.

He grinned broadly and mumbled under his breath, "She's driving me crazy. She's the sexiest woman I've seen in a very long time. I have to get to know her. Really well."

Jake noticed the encounter between Bea and Nick. "What in the hell is that sneaky fella sayin to Bea? He'd best stick to his business and leave her alone." Jake felt a strange stirring in his body, one he hadn't allowed himself to feel for years.

Ed walked to the band, lined up in parade fashion, drum major poised with a baton, cheerleaders behind him. "It's two o'clock straight up. Blow your whistle, loud." Ed gave the start sign, ran to the back of the line and jumped in his Mercury. Bea joined the onlookers, and the festivities began.

Signs routed traffic to a parking area next to the high school sports field. Both sides of the block making up El Chico's business district, were packed with people. Those who wanted close-up views arrived early that morning and staked out places to sit. Children assembled on blankets in front of their parents, who were in lawn chairs or standing in groups.

"Here they come!" Ethel Ogletree was with the high-rise apartment group.

"You're blocking my view," said one of her neighbors, trying to see over the maze of flowers on top of her straw hat.

"Here, I'll just step to the side and you can see better." Ethel tiptoed to her right, careful not to stab a child with her spiked heels.

"Oh, there they are. Heeyyyy Etta!" Turning back to her friend she continued talking. "Aren't they just elegant?"

Minnie Lee Gibbons strained to see the mayor and his wife on the back of the Cadillac. "And, look at that! One of those fancy sports cars."

"Yes, that's Nicholas Graystone's. He drove it all the way from Dallas for the parade. I'd say he is one gorgeous man." Lulu Belle waved and Nick waved back. "Ohhhh! Did you see that, girls? He waved to me."

Cheers and comments continued among the spectators as the band marched by, wearing red shirts and hats with the Horn Toad logo embroidered in iridescent thread. Next, a variety of leashed dogs, from Dachshunds to Heinz 57s, followed their owners. The canines and people were dressed in clown outfits.

"Oh my Lord." Lulu screamed. "Here comes Joe Ray, I mean, Jose`. He's a real Vaquero. Did you ever see anyone throw a lasso like he's doing?" The crowd cheered as they watched the Tejano caballero stand on his horse and twirl two ropes around his body, pull them in, sit back in the saddle and continue riding in the parade. "That man is a real surprise. He has talent."

Chester and his wife, in their shiny waxed Gremlin, honked and tossed candy, garnering some applause. Wilmur White in his minivan, with "White's General Mercantile and Grocery Store" written on the side, made his way around the parade route. A huge speaker mounted on the top broadcast his daughter, Clarajean, singing a series of country western songs.

"Hey Jake!" A 4H member's dad and mom waved and whistled as Jake and his tractor pulled the school-aged kids along the parade route. The kids threw rubber balls into the crowd, creating a scrambling match. Jake tipped his hat and smiled broadly at Bea when he passed her. She returned his greeting with a wink.

Little boys were wide-eyed, babies cried, and parents grabbed their small children making sure they were out of the way when Juan Martinez and Big Al Mosley's eighteen-wheeler rolled past. They were followed by Dalton Darnell's official sheriff car, with its lights flashing and siren blasting. Doug Farnsworth drove the town's fire truck with Herb Matson and Oliver Brumfeld dressed in full firefighting regalia balanced on the back, holding onto Ten-Four who sported a firefighting dog vest and hat. Large signs mounted on both sides reminded the crowd about the festival, food, bazaar, and dance.

Ed Hawkins ended the parade in his Mercury. When he arrived at the school he could see that somehow the parade-parking plan had not been followed. The lead car, driven by Lester with the mayor and his wife back seat driving, was parked in the center of the circular drive leaving little room for the following parade vehicles. Cars, floats and people were everywhere, scattered like a mass of pick-up sticks. He hoped no one would need to leave fast, because it would be impossible.

THE FESTIVAL

The sweating spectators made their way to the high school's back lawn where rows of tents were set up, housing tables stacked with homemade food, arts and crafts. The longest lines were for cold drinks. Families spread blankets or set up tables. Some brought their own picnic lunches with them, but most purchased plates piled high with Billy's barbecue and Dolly's salad.

"Even in this heat the brisket's delicious." Chester and Violet sat with Wilmur and Gaylene White.

"Chester, your car was one of the best in the parade," said Gaylene.

"And Clarajean is as pretty and talented as any of those stars on Grand Ole Opry, or American Idol," replied Violet.

"I'll second that," added Chester.

Bea and Ed huddled in a corner discussing the challenging parking situation.

"Hello, there." Graystone approached the two with cold drinks in hand. "It looks like y'all could use some cool refreshment."

Bea smiled and accepted the cup. "Thank you, Nick,"

He flashed his most winning smile.

"I've got to be goin. I promised the wife I'd meet her fifteen minutes ago. So, I'll let you enjoy your drinks." Ed walked away, leaving Bea with her admirer.

She wanted to strangle Ed for deserting her, but the Dallasite *was* charming.

"I've seen you at all the town meetings and understand from Percy that you're not only the secretary for the council, but also a reporter for the paper."

Bea sipped her drink and nodded her head.

"And, Bea, you're a rancher in addition to your city jobs?"

"Yes, I own the Circle McP about five miles out of town. We're cattle ranchers but lately that doesn't amount to much."

Continuing to smile and speaking in a soft voice, he leaned down to Bea. "How about joining me over at the barbecue booth? I'd like to get your perspective about the drought and how it's effecting your business and El Chico."

Bea made her way beside Graystone to a picnic table. Across the school yard, Jake watched, a scowl on his face. He thought he and Bea would spend the afternoon together enjoying the festival, and there she was with the big city phony.

"Hi, Jake." Clarajean and two of her girlfriends greeted him. "Come and get some of Billy's brisket with us. You just *have* to see us perform with the band. We've been rehearsin for weeks."

Jake smiled and did as the girls asked. *What else do I have to do?* He pouted to himself.

The temperature dropped to an almost comfortable level as the sun lowered on the horizon. Ladies filled shopping bags with the handmade bazaar items while the men discussed the lack of business and their political views.

"Herb, Herb!" Mary Nelle searched the crowd for her husband, finally locating him in a cluster of locals. "Where's our car? I've looked high and low for it. I need to put my bags up before the dance starts."

"Hmmmmm." Herb looked around the schoolyard. In the maze of vehicles he wasn't sure where he parked. "Sweetheart," he always called her that when he knew things were not going well, "Just put the bags under a table and we'll find the car later."

That conversation was repeated over and over again by attendees who misplaced their rides. So, stacks of bags, purses and hats were piled under trees, in corners or under tables ready to pick up at the end of the celebration.

The dance band, made of part of the parade group plus Mabel Pevey on the keyboard, Gertrude Whitfield on fiddle, Billy Nelson on guitar, and Jose` on the drums, began playing. Clarajean White sang and people swirled in time with the music. Children danced with each other, their parents or grandparents. Couples who hadn't done the two-step for years scooted around the outdoor basketball court having the most fun they'd shared in a very long time.

Jake's scowl turned to a full-fledged frown as he watched Graystone swing Bea around like they were a regular couple.

"Bea, you are quite a good dancer." Graystone twirled her under his arm, grabbled her artfully with his other and do-si-doed her around and around the dance floor.

In spite of herself, she was having a good time. "You aren't so bad yourself." Bea smiled at the man. She felt Jake's eyes on her so she turned and waved. He was in the center of what looked like the entire cheerleading squad and football team. He turned his head as if he didn't see her.

Once Bea and Nick were sitting again, he began questioning her about her ranch, its history, and her role as owner-manager. "It seems to me that you've been tied down to that ranch for 'way too long. Maybe one day soon you can get away for a few days and join me in Dallas for a football game and dinner."

Bea smiled. "You must know that I disagree with the entire concept of the pipeline project."

"Yeah. I guessed that from the looks you gave me at the meetings. Maybe when you're in Dallas I can show you my firm's office and photos of similar projects. Perhaps then you'll be convinced the pipeline is the way to go."

"We'll see." Bea looked the man in the eyes. "We'll see."

Jake said good-bye to the teens surrounding him and sauntered over to Bea and her companion. "Good evenin, Bea."

Bea jumped at the sound of his voice. "Hi Jake. Nick, this is Jake Johnson. You might remember each other from the town meeting."

"Yes, I remember you." Jake did not hide his contempt.

Graystone unfolded his six and a half foot frame, straightened his shirt sleeves and extended his hand, looking down at Jake. "It's a pleasure. Bea told me all about your work at *her* ranch." The tone of his voice was condescending.

"Yeah. I've been at the Circle McP since Bea was a teenager and we've been friends all these years. She's very special."

"I agree with you on that point. She's special indeed."

"I promised her parents I'd always look after her, so, it's important for you to know that's a fact you'll have to deal with.

"Well, Jack... or is it Jake? He continued to look down at the man. "It looks like Bea is plenty capable of taking care of herself. Aren't you, Bea?" He placed his hand on her shoulder.

Bea got up and took a few steps back from the men. "I think it's time for me to say good night to both of you. It's been a long day."

"Look, Graystone, I don't know who you think you are in big ol' Dallas, but here, you're just another city slicker who don't fit in. I, for one, don't trust a thing you're doin about the drought situation. I think the pipeline idea is bad and know your reputation is shit. I'd like to see you stay where you belong, far from here."

Graystone's eyes narrowed, his face turned bright red. "Cowboy, you better stay out of my way when I'm here. I'll see Bea whenever I can. You have no idea who I am."

Having overheard the argument, the mayor joined in. "Jake, you're out of line here. The whole town thinks the pipeline is a great idea and that it'll save our city."

"Well, I wouldn't say 'everyone.' I, for one, have my doubts about it." Doug Farnsworth joined the expanding circle of men.

"Gentlemen, I assure you that with my guidance your little town will be reborn." Nick stepped forward reaching for Bea. He put his arm around her and gave her a big hug. "This pretty lady here can help put the whole thing together, can't you, hon?" He looked into her eyes and smiled.

Jake's fist flew through the air as fast as a fish going after a well-baited line. It landed on the man's jaw and sent him reeling. On his way down, Graystone swiped at Jake but missed. Bea screamed and the group of high school boys who'd been sitting with Jake bound across the tables as if called to battle. They circled the downed man, daring him to make a move. Adult men joined in the exchange, some punching anyone close and others grabbing the boys to prevent a full-on bloody war. Ed Hawkins and the sheriff blew whistles, pulled scuffling men apart and herded the boys away.

Women, afraid they would lose their day's purchases, scurried around like ants, adding their shrill cries to the mix. They pulled their belonging from their hiding places and ran to the parking lot. They resembled rats looking for a piece of cheese in a maze. A traffic jam, similar to one on a Houston freeway resulted, with horns honking and rude finger gestures rampant. Tempers in El Chico reached a crescendo. In the pandemonium, Jake turned around and strolled away, Bea was the only one who noticed.

Nick straightened his clothes, apologizing and consoling. "Bea. I'm sorry for any ungentlemanly behavior on my part. Sometimes things get out of hand in this extreme heat." The two walked to his car, easy to spot in the main school driveway. He took her hand. "Thank you, Bea for a lovely day. I truly like you, want to get to know you better. If it's okay, I'd like to call you next week."

Bea was puzzled. Nick wasn't at all what she expected. He was fun, nice, and even kind. She *would* like to get to know him better. Maybe she'd take him up on his invitation and see him the next time she was in Dallas.

She kicked the ground as she walked back to the remains of the festival. "Just wait 'til I get my hands on that damn Jake Johnson! He is in a deep pile of shit." Looking around at what was left of the festival, she joined Ed, who was helping the few remaining committee members take down tents, gather garbage, and count the dollars collected.

"Well, darlin, that was some way to end Founders Day. I don't know what Graystone or Jake said, but it was somethin if it got grown men to let loose like that. I guess everyone's tempers were on edge anyway. This was just the match that lit the fuse."

ADVICE

"That was quite a blow you gave Graystone." Silver Crow rode beside Jake as they made their way across the prairie on horseback.

"Damn it, Crow. From the git-go I didn't like the man. Something's not right with him, plus he's makin a big play for Bea and she's fallin for him."

"Yeah, and you don't care a thing about Bea in a romantic way, right?"

"Don't push me or you'll get the same slug that smug greenhorn got."

Silver Crow teased. "It's your own fault if you let someone besides you romance Bea. Why don't you just admit you love her and get on with it?"

"That's enough. Even if it's true, she don't think of me that way."

"Don't be so sure about that, cowboy. Just give some thought to why she's passed up so many opportunities all these years." The two men rode on.

Silver Crow turned slightly in the saddle. "I told you I'd look into Graystone's background, and I did. I didn't find anything specific, but no one over in Austin trusts him. He did nothin useful when he was on the Water Board. He's a complete ass unless he's trying to sell some deal. An ol boy over in Lubbock says his brother-in-law paid H_2O a down payment on a shopping center project and when the deal fell apart Graystone kept all the money. They didn't sue, but my friend thought the whole thing stunk."

"Let's keep on diggin. I know we're gonna find some criminal dealings that involve this blowhard. Meanwhile, Bea's so mad at me

I don't dare mention the guy's name around her. All we talk about is ranch business, like we're strictly business partners. It's never been like this between us. I think she'll see him when she's in Dallas later this month and I cain't do a thing about it."

MORE CRIME

Shorter days and somewhat lower temperatures hinted to the citizens that it was autumn. There was still no sign of rain and opinions about constructing a water pipeline continued to polarize El Chico's residents. A few were for collecting higher taxes on the rich, but the vast majority of voters wanted no tax increases for any reason. Neighbors with differing opinions didn't speak to each other and sat on opposite sides at church. It didn't help that each Sunday brought a different visiting minister, who had no idea about the town's problems, to the Methodist Church.

Dalton Darnell waved goodbye to Dolly and Billy Nelson. The sheriff was one of the regulars at On the Road Again. He returned the Stetson to his head and sauntered out the door.

Dalton drank coffee all day to stay awake while he checked with the bank, the grocery store, and the other businesses along Main Street to be sure all was safe. He was glad the little township was a peaceful place but his days were so boring he daydreamed about robbing the bank himself for excitement.

The last crime they had, if he didn't count the girl-fight at Lulu Belle's or the fist exchange between Jake and the honcho from Dallas, was when the Farnsworth Truck Stop and Cafe was robbed.

For the past fifteen years, the sheriff began each workday by guiding his Harley through the five blocks of town ending at the old two-story Texas Ranger Building out on the highway. The city shared office space with the El Chico Motel. Buzzie and Annie Adams lived upstairs in a loft area. The motel and law enforcement offices covered the downstairs.

The huge, barnlike building was on the Texas Historical Commission's list and had a brass plaque posted left of the big oak door to prove it. The three-foot thick walls were native stone and the inside was decorated with dozens of scruffy, old, but once-award-winning wild game trophies, all staring down from the eighteen-foot high mesquite ceilings. The only heat for the blustery winters came from a giant fireplace, large enough for a man to stand inside.

The long row of motel rooms was built in the 1950s and honored the original Texas Rangers. Each door was adorned with a brass star engraved with the name of one of the famed heroes. Framed photos and typewritten histories of each ranger's contributions to the taming of Texas were hung on the walls.

Some motel guests, usually hunters or families coming to bury relatives in the nearby cemetery, complained the wallpaper, towels, and chenille bedspreads dated back to the 1800s. Locals knew that wasn't true because when Buzzie and Annie took the place over in the late 1980s, they redecorated.

Half a football field behind the motel rooms, gigantic pieces of the unassembled water tower were scattered around the side of the mountain. The place looked more like a junkyard than Ed's salvage business.

Buzzie and Annie served as deputies and each received a small sum from the city in consideration of their aid imposing the laws of the great state of Texas. Buzzie, like Dalton, hoped someday they'd have a real case to follow. Meanwhile, they took pride in staying up-to-date with law enforcement practices by attending classes and by making friends with the Highway Patrol officers in their county.

When town revenues were down, Dalton and Buzzie took turns hiding behind the giant billboard southeast of town that announced in faded letters, "WELCOME TO EL CHICO, HOME OF THE FIGHTING HORN TOADS." They aimed radar guns at naïve drivers who took the picturesque route that went through the center of El

Chico. The tourists rarely saw the small sign changing the speed limit from 65 to 35.

"Makes them easy pickins for us. If a driver happens to be swiggin some Lone Star, that's even better for El Chico's budget," said Dalton when he explained to the city council why the jail, a small stone relic left over from the Ranger era was used to house drunk drivers overnight.

The lawbreakers were required to face County Judge, Samuel S. "Snake" Lambert. The man was legendary and held court in the main room of the sheriff's office. Surrounded by the mounted trophies, glass eyes intimidating detainees, the "Snake" issued verdicts on an as-needed-on-call basis. Prisoners quickly sobered up and paid, anxious to get back on the highway and out of El Chico.

On this particular day, as Dalton strolled down the sidewalk on his way to his next stop, the First State Bank of El Chico, he daydreamed about chatting with the teller, Angelina Broadmere. He never tired of Angelina, mesmerized by her topaz eyes, longest eyelashes and the biggest chest he'd ever seen.

The sheriff was finger-brushing his goatee when Buzzie drove up beside him, brakes squealing, motioning for him to get in the car. "There's been a robbery at Lulu Belle's Boutique," shouted the deputy. He hit the siren and gunned the 1989 Ford's engine. So far, the old rod had outrun every challenger and it was still going strong.

The deputy slammed on the brakes when they reached the store and both Dalton and Buzzie jumped out, leaving the car lights flashing. They ran through the open door into the shop. Ladies' clothing, jewelry and handbags were thrown here and there, covering the floor.

Lulu Belle sat near a mound of hangers and garments shaking and crying, mascara staining her rosy cheeks. "They robbed me! Just look at everything."

"Are you okay? Are they still around?" shouted Dalton, pistol out of his holster.

"I'm okay. Don't know where they are," she hiccupped. "We've hardly ever had this kind of thing happen in El Chico."

"Now, now, Lulu," soothed Buzzie. "Let's calm down."

"Tell us all about it." The sheriff returned his pistol to its holster, notepad in hand.

"They had me lay down on the floor and said not to move for an hour or they'd shoot me."

A case at last, the sheriff thought.

For the next half-hour Dalton listened to Lulu recap the incident while Buzzie used their new fingerprinting kit. "Now, as I understand it, you opened the "Be Lovely Boutique" at ten and just as you opened the door two ladies entered right behind you."

"Well, they wasn't ladies if you ask me," said Lulu. "They grabbed me, covered my head with this here bag and shoved me down behind the desk," she sobbed again and caught her breath. "They said they needed some up-to-date fashion and heard I had some."

"So, they wanted clothes? Not money?" asked Buzzie.

"One was askin for a red dress and got mad 'cause she didn't find one. The other woman said she heard we had lots of sexy evenin outfits and then they started cussin at each other. I cain't remember much except it was so scary. It all happened so quick!"

On the interview went, with the two men questioning Lulu and searching for evidence.

"No, I don't know if they was black or white. Or young or old. I'm not sure what they took since they was yellin at each other sayin they didn't like my style." Lulu's tears and cries grew stronger. "They didn't even like my selections when they was stealin them!"

A couple of hours later, Lulu Belle and the Be Lovely Boutique were put back in order with Deputy Annie and Bea McPherson's help. Bea stopped by to get information and take pictures for a feature in the *El Chico Times Gazette*.

A frustrated sheriff paced up and down, flipping through his notebook. He moaned, "Lulu, this is a difficult situation for us in law enforcement. We ain't sure anything was taken, there ain't no fingerprints, don't know a thing about the robbers, and you're fine. It looks like we don't have much of a case."

The front page of the EL Chico newspaper was covered with a huge photo of Lulu flanked by the sheriff and his deputy. The headline read, "Fashionable Crime." Townspeople were outraged that one of their own had been harmed and soon neighbors were speaking again, banding together against mutual foes. Any change from drought conditions and the pipeline argument was a welcome diversion.

"Nick, you didn't have anything to do with the newest robbery in El Chico, did you?" Percy called Graystone as soon as he heard about the Be Lovely robbery.

"Now Percy. Why would you think that? Land purchases are going well, thanks to you and the weather, but you have to admit a robbery like that one might help move the downtown property purchases along." He leaned over Janelle's desk and gave her a nod, putting his hand over the receiver, he whispered, "It worked."

Janelle smiled and grabbed her handbag and mouthed, "Let's go and celebrate."

TAXES OR PRAYER

Bea's white Escalade was parked in front of Ed's Salvage Yard and Golf Course. Ed and Bea sat under the row of trees on the back fairway sipping iced tea and talking about the Be Lovely robbery and other city gossip.

"Ed, you know I have concerns about the pipeline idea and about Nick Graystone. You're the only one I know I can trust to keep what I have to say confidential."

"You never have to worry about me being your friend, Bea. Sometimes it's just good to get things off your chest, so talk and I'll listen." Ed pulled his chair closer as the two sat.

"Even if the pipeline is a viable plan, El Chico would empty its treasury and have to assess unreasonable taxes to pay for it."

Ed nodded in agreement.

"More than that, I'm really puzzled why the Circle McP has a tiny bit of a stream coming from the spring close to the barn. If the aquifer was dry, wouldn't all the springs stop producing?"

"Bea, you saw all the reports Graystone showed us and it sure looks like the acquifer's done. The town is dying on the vine, and you're right on target about the pipeline being impossible. The town needs to get back on its feet somehow and that's gonna take some big-time rain. There's nothin we can do about that."

"That's not exactly right. We could ask Silver Crow to do the ceremony. It might not work, but then again, the native people got along for centuries with these rituals. Why wouldn't we do this? I just don't understand."

"Sure you do, Bea. We couldn't ask for better-intentioned people to have as neighbors, but sometimes they're stuck in a murky mire of guilt and fear taught in some churches. I don't think that's what the Bible is about, but we're up against lots of people who've bought into the interpertitions of a few rigid religious leaders."

"We have a new preacher starting at the Methodist Church and I think he might think like you and I do, keeping the main thing about love, forgiveness, helping our fellow man … and being flexible about the rest of it. Maybe he'll be able to bring about a change."

Bea sipped her tea. "Ed, I also came to talk with you about the tower. I've seen how much it means to the town. It's the first thing that has given some hope to El Chico, so I want us to finish the project. We have to replace all the pumping mechanisms regardless."

"Yeah, Bea. I agree, but we're well short of the money to finish the work. Founder's Day wasn't enough."

"I know. And I, along with my brother, want to provide whatever it takes to get this thing up and full so we get some water pressure again."

"Now, Bea, you can't mean it. You have a ranch to think about, your own problems and such."

"Ed, no one around here knows how much I won in Las Vegas and how much Harold's investments have paid off for us, but it's plenty. I want to do something to help but don't want anyone but you to know about it, not even Odelia."

Ed and Bea continued to talk, agreeing there would be an anonymous donation they could say was part of Founder's Day. Bea would get money wired to a county seat bank, pick up cash from them and then Ed would deposit it into El Chico's general account.

Within a week, Ed and his crew were working daily at the edge of the mountain, erecting the gigantic El Chico tower and updating the rusted pumping system. Everyone assumed Founder's Day provided the needed funds.

It was Friday and the Be Lovely Boutique had metamorphosed into the Cut 'n Curl.

"I'm so sorry I behaved like I did over the pipeline project." Ethel hugged Lulu. "It's just too exciting to see the water tower going up, up, and up."

"It is truly a fine sight. Bunches of truckers we've never seen before are stopping for gas and pie and want to know all about it." Wilma Farnsworth drank a glass of lemonade as she visited with her friends. "They think the tower is putting El Chico back on the map.

"There's just nothin as important as us sticking together and helpin each other in times of need. I cain't tell each of you how much your friendship has meant while I get my treatments." Juanita Gutierrez was having her nails done surrounded by the town ladies, bald head covered with a trendy scarf supplied by Lulu.

"Seein you look better is the answer to prayer and a tribute to modern medicine," said Ethel, hanging a blue hat with purple flowers on the rack.

"Thanks, Ethel. I'm feelin so much better and the doctors are very encouragin. I wish all my hair hadn't fell out but someday it'll grow back."

"Fightin over an ol pipeline is not a good use of our energy when there are more important things, like illnesses and love, to be concerned about." Odelia was helping out by being manicurist for the day while Lulu rested in the swivel chair, still in shock over the robbery. Bea stood behind the distraught woman and massaged her shoulders.

"Bea, I have to ask you. What was up with Jake and that Dallas guy? It looked like maybe Jake was jealous when you were dancin." Odelia's question was one the entire group had wanted to ask for weeks but they'd hung back, knowing Bea never shared anything private.

"Yes, Bea," Lulu turned around in the chair. "I've thought Jake was sweet on you for years and it's real plain that Mr. Dallas has a huge crush on you."

"Now, ladies," Bea continued her massaging. "Jake and I've been friends forever and Graystone, well, it's true he is interested and interesting. I'll just have to see what happens. Right now all I have time for is work."

The ladies giggled. "I think we have a love triangle going on. This could be fun." Lulu swiveled back.

Etta Ruth squinted, turning her eyes into mere slits over her mountainous cheeks. She didn't like the thought of Bea McPherson being in the limelight with Nick Graystone for *any* reason. She was the mayor's wife, and inside her envious mind she reasoned that she, not Bea, should have the Dallas man's attention.

"I think we have other things to talk about." Bea laughed, trying to divert the focus of the conversation. "The tower is going up and that's a huge step for us. But, this town's men don't seem to have an ounce of common sense about what to do next to keep El Chico alive. Some don't want to face the fact it would empty our treasury to pay even a part of the pipeline project. There might be nothin we can do to get water but pray, and maybe ask Silver Crow about his ceremony. That would cost us zero dollars and it certainly can't hurt."

"Well, don't you think it is sacrilegious to have some non-Christian ceremony?" Etta Ruth looked around the room to see what the other women thought. Her face had turned red and her head was plastered with black dye making her look like a frightening cartoon character. "I can't believe y'all are even talking about this. Percy and I are one hundred percent behind the pipeline, want nothin to do with the Indian ceremony, and think each of us can make more sacrifices to get the pipeline started." Etta knew her husband would be very upset about the tone of this discussion. Their secret plans for the resort and land acquisitions were well underway. Just yesterday she signed papers buying another small parcel adjacent to the mountain.

"Well, I certainly don't approve of any heathen ceremony," said Ethel Ogletree, popping out from under the dryer. "Jesus Christ said he is the only Lord and Savior right in the Bible."

"Yes, but he also said man is to help himself. I don't see a conflict. The ceremony would focus our thoughts about rain and water in a special kind of prayer." Bea stopped massaging and stepped to the center of the room. "It can't be any worse than taking good, hard-earned money and throwing it at a pipeline that we aren't sure about. Now, maybe once Mr. Graystone proves we could actually pump water seventy miles, and gets the rights-of-way and such, then, maybe we could begin thinking about how to pay for it."

"I think we have to do everything we can and do it together, none of this fighting among us. That will not please the Lord or accomplish anything." Lulu stood up.

"I'm going to talk to Wilmur White and Oliver Brumfeld personally to see if I can change their minds about the ceremony," Wilma added. "It can't hurt."

"Ed already wants to do it," said Odelia.

Her voice shrill and loud, Etta Ruth grabbed her oversized handbag planning to leave. " Bea, since you're so smitten with Nick, why don't you get some more proof about the project and then maybe you'll start makin good sense. I cain't believe any of you would take a chance on offending the Lord by havin Silver Crow's ceremony."

"Now, bless your heart, Etta Ruth. You've gone and lost your temper so bad you forgot that your head is full of raven dye. Sit down and breathe deep while I fix your hair fit for a mayor's wife." Lulu pointed to the reclined chair by the sink. "Now sit."

REAL ESTATE

"This is the check for our operating expenses, Nick. It's made out to you just like you asked." Percy ushered his partner into his and Etta's parlor.

After Graystone pocketed the check, he grinned knowing the couple would be inclined to invest even more of their personal funds once they saw the official looking architectural drawings he was unfolding. "This is a rendering of the health spa connected to the back of the resort. You'll see a series of small soaking pools in a garden setting. The mountain will be a great backdrop."

"It's just beautiful, Nick." Etta Ruth fluttered her lashes and smiled at the man as she laid plates full of sandwiches, chips and cupcakes beside the full silver coffee service that was prepared for their guest.

"Oh, Etta, thanks, but I can't stay long. I hope you didn't go to a lot of trouble on my behalf." The man managed a forlorn look as he watched disappointment travel like a dark cloud across the woman's face.

"Sure, Nick. I should have known you'd be busy. It's really nothing."

"Maybe next time. I'll need to come back in a couple of weeks to get another check for the operating fund. All these plans are costing us but I'm sure you'll agree it's well worth it to be prepared."

Percy shrugged his shoulders and began thumbing through the plans. "I like it. Just like I told you on the phone last week, I bought two new properties on the northeast side of the mountain perfect for this part of the resort. The owners were sick of the drought and just wanted out. It was too good an opportunity to pass up."

"If you're sure all these acquisitions are confidential, that no one knows who the West Pecos Corporation is, it's okay. If the word got out we are the principals we'd be in deep trouble. That goes for anything else we're doin. You got that?" Nick gave the Mayor a threatening look, folded up the papers and put them in his briefcase. "Any word about the Farnsworth place? Or any of the downtown strip?"

"Nope. Those are going to be hard ones. Doug and Wilma aren't interested in selling; seem content as well-fed milk cows. We've already bought all the vacant downtown spaces on the east side. Lulu Belle Schwartz and the Whites are holding on, even after the robbery."

""Like I told you before, Percy, once we have the land we need under contract, we can get one of the big Dallas or Houston banks to back the project. You might already know that I have Miss McPherson visiting me in Dallas next week. I'm going to mention the idea of me personally purchasing the Circle McP Ranch. If we could get that, we'd have control of El Chico and the total area surrounding the mountain."

The mayor nodded in agreement.

"Meanwhile, we have to keep very quiet, avoid talking about property sales. Do you both understand?" Nick stared into Etta's eyes.

Etta smiled and sighed. "Of course I would never say a word about anything you want to be secret, Nick." She had been afraid Nick was interested in Bea for something other than land and now she knew the truth, or thought she did. In her opinion the ranch woman didn't deserve any more admiration than she already had.

"You've always been able to count on me. I'm already acting like a damn CIA operative." Percy broke out in sweat. "I must level with you. The council will meet next week and I know the vote for upping taxes is not going to pass. They're all involved in getting the water tower built."

"Glad to hear the tower is keeping troublemakers busy." Nick stood up, preparing to leave, his demeanor no longer friendly, but as cool as a complete stranger's. The overweight couple scurried to match the tall man's lead to the door.

"Don't worry about the tax vote, Nick. In the long run, those against us can't make much of an impact one way or another."

"Whoever's left in El Chico after we secure these properties will have to sell out or join up. El Chico is dead without us. But, you two understand in no uncertain terms, if any of this gets out I'll deny any knowledge of it. I'd be forced to do some things I wouldn't want to do. Get it?"

Etta Ruth squeezed her husband's hand. For a brief moment she questioned their involvement with Nicholas Graystone.

BEA AND NICK

"Harold, we need to talk, right away." Bea left the message on her brother's voice mail and waited. She was sitting alone in her living room, back home from her trip to Dallas.

Nick had invited her to stay in his palatial Highland Park home but she refused, making her own reservation at a Holiday Inn. She was amazed when he had a limo pick her up for dinner. Nick met her with a single red rose in his hand. The Inn on Turtle Creek Restaurant was more upscale than any dining experience she remembered. He was a perfect gentleman, charming her with his undivided attention. They went to the symphony and then out for a late dessert.

When they returned to the hotel he held her hand as they walked into the lobby. He bent down and lightly kissed her. "Be ready at nine sharp tomorrow, dear Bea. My car will pick you up early for a full day of fun."

Wow, not what I expected. He's quite a guy. So interesting. Her lips still tingled from his kiss. Bea sighed as she tucked herself in bed propped up on a mass of pillows. As she stared at the ceiling, she reconstructed their conversation in her mind. It had centered on business outlooks, current news, and Texas gossip. His kiss? Well, it said nothing about business.

The next morning, Nick insisted on showing her his home and having a fancy-dressed maid serve them brunch. Then they went to his office. The place was upscale but Bea was surprised when the only employee present was his assistant.

"It's so nice to finally meet you, Bea. Nick has said so many great things about you." Jaynell shook Bea's hand. "I'm so sorry no one else is here to meet you. Everyone is in the field or working from home."

Bea was impressed with the short tour that included Nick's corner office. Then he drove Bea around Dallas pointing out various landmarks; where the football stadium was and where he played golf.

Just before she headed back to El Chico, they enjoyed a casual mid-afternoon snack at a trendy restaurant. Nick reached across the table and took her hand. "Bea, we've talked about everything but your ideas for the future. I'd like to know about the ranch and what you plan to do with the rest of your life." No men, other than Harold and Jake, had talked with her about personal dreams in many years and she wasn't sure how to respond.

"Look, Nick. I'm not sure what you're wantin to know. What you see is what I am, a small-time rancher from a little town in west Texas, nothing more. The ranch was my parents', and my dad's parents' before them. It's in my blood. My family includes my brother and his wife, who live in California; my dog, several cats, a few cattle, the sheep and goats and some chickens. My goals are pretty simple. I want to get through the drought in good enough shape to restart my herd."

"I'm surprised your brother isn't running the Circle McP. Why is that?"

As Nick listened attentively, Bea explained about Harold and how she was the one who loved ranching from the beginning, not her brother.

"Bea, Bea, Bea. I look at you and see a smart, savvy woman, beautiful and maybe wasting away out there in the boonies. I know you love your ranch and the open spaces, but I also see how hard you work. Don't you ever want more? Maybe like Harold? Maybe the ability to experience something like in the past day, a touch of life in a city?"

Bea was speechless.

"Don't let me shock you, but I'm a man who speaks what's on his mind. I was attracted to you the first time I saw you at the town meeting."

She still couldn't think of a thing to say so she just stared at the man.

"I've been thinking about a business idea for you. Bea, it's just something for you to contemplate now and maybe consider sometime down the line. Your property is prime real estate in that part of Texas, what with it backing up to that mountain. You said it has a slight water supply. We both know someday you'll have water again because someday it will rain again. What if you forgot about a working cattle ranch, other than as a small side-business, and made your spread into a dude ranch?"

Bea's mouth dropped open. "That's ridiculous, Nick. Who ever heard of such a thing in El Chico, or in our county, for that matter? And, I don't know anything about dude ranches. I'd hate havin a bunch of strangers roaming around my land."

"Well, I see that I've upset you and I apologize. I'm a businessman, Bea, and I'm always thinking about business. Forgive me for being so blunt about my idea. But with El Chico running out of water and the whole place dying out, maybe this idea will be one you'll consider in the future. I'd be a very interested investor in such a project. Just think about it, okay?"

"Nick, I don't want to think about it. I'm still hoping El Chico will pull out of this slump and I can have a successful ranch again. I appreciate your business experience and admire your success, but me, I'm just a country girl."

Graystone smiled and took her hand again. "Let's talk about more pleasant things. Tell me about the ranch's history and I'll tell you about how I got into football." The two shared stories, laughing together. When they finished their food and drinks, he walked her to her car.

He opened the door and pulled Bea to him, encircling her in his arms. Then, as if she would break, he pushed a strand of hair away from her face and kissed her softly on the mouth. He brushed her lips with his fingers causing Bea to shiver. He continued with a series of small kisses, each growing with intensity until the couple was engaged in a full, lingering, and passionate mouth-to-mouth embrace. Her heart was pounding. She could feel his body responding. Then, he took her shoulders in his large hands and pushed her away, smiling and gazing into her eyes.

"Oh God. I didn't expect this. Bea, you are really something special." He took a deep breath and shook his head. He helped her into the driver's seat and shut the car door. "Please take care of yourself. Drive safe. I'll call you and be hoping to see you very soon."

★ ★ ★

Bea raced back to El Chico as fast as she could without attracting the attention of the Texas Highway Patrol. She thought about Nick, how handsome and gallant he was. Remembering his kisses and the feel of his body against hers sent chills up her arms and legs. She knew she was sexually attracted to him but maybe the attraction had more to do with her loneliness than with the man himself. Why had she waited around for Jake for so many years? The cowboy would never change and she was sick of being alone.

She turned her radio up, flipping from one station to another, listening to every program she could get, hoping to block out the feel of Nick's kisses and body. She tried to focus on what he had said about the Circle McP. The sad truth was that his idea, as depressing as it was, might someday be the route she'd have to take with her property. Tears filled her eyes as she thought about the demise of her cattle herd, the dried up grassland and the end of the independent Texas ranch era.

★ ★ ★

When Harold returned Bea's call, she related the Dallas experience to her big brother. "Bea, this Graystone guy sounds like he's making a lot of sense to me. It does concern me he's coming on to you a bit fast, but then, that's the way some men behave when they're accustomed to being in charge. What does Jake think about this?"

"I've hardly talked with Jake lately and I'd never tell him about being with Nick." Bea then told Harold about the fight on Founder's Day.

"That doesn't sound like Jake. I've trusted him completely for most of our lives. Have you ever thought he might care for you in a romantic way and that he was jealous? Frankly Bea, I've never been able to figure out yours and Jake's relationship. I know you've had a crush on Jake all your life and I've suspected he feels the same way but just not able to tell you."

"Don't be ridiculous! We're best friends, or were. I don't know what to think about Nick but I do know what I'm feelin.'"

"Well, sometimes feelings can get ve-rrrry confusing. I think you should think long and hard about both men before doing anything impulsive. Meanwhile, I know Jake's intuition is the best. I'm positive he is looking out for you. Maybe he doesn't trust Graystone for a good reason."

"I can't imagine why, other than he doesn't like anything new. I was skeptical myself until I got to know Nick."

"Sis, I'm just saying, sometimes we know you can be a bit hotheaded. Just take this romance thing slowly. Be sure, or as sure as anyone can be when love is involved."

"You're right. I may be acting on passion and not using good common sense." Bea paused and took a deep breath. "Until now I didn't remember, but, Harold, I have some charts Nick accidentally dropped when he left the town meeting back in the spring. I'm going to find them just to be sure about the water rights and such. Why don't I sent copies to you to look over?"

"Now you're thinking, little sis. First of all, how about you taking it easy, don't do anything but relax and think about this dude ranch idea as one option for your future. Meanwhile, I'm going to do a little research of my own."

"Harold, I don't know what I'd do without you. I'm in over my head."

"Bea, I'm sorry. For years I haven't been there for you. You seemed so capable. I ignored the signs that you needed some help. I'm on board now and will do all I can for you, the ranch and El Chico."

COUNCIL MEETING

"Quiet, quiet!" The mayor slammed his gavel on the ancient oak table in the town library, where they were holding the council meeting. "Will everybody just shut up? We all have time to express our opinions, but let's do it one at a time. Councilman Lester Plunker is here to give us a first-hand report."

"Thanks, Mayor." Lester stood up and straightened his well-worn suit and tie. "I know I'm bringin up church business at a government meeting but this is something that will effect our community as a whole. The council should know in case the whole town goes berserk."

"So are we goin to be invaded by terrorists?" The mayor joked, but behind the façade he was concerned. He and Graystone didn't need any legal trouble now that they were near the finish line of their project.

"No, but it's similar. The Methodist bishops have appointed a minister to replace Brother Pevey," continued Lester.

"That sounds like great news." Ed Hawkins leaned back in his chair.

"Now mind you, the new Reverend is here on a trial basis, but it is quite upsetting to learn they have sent a Negra man to El Chico to stand in the pulpit. I can't imagine his chances of staying here permanent are good, but he's here for awhile anyway." Lester looked around the table at the shocked faces.

"Well now, that is news. Old man Washington and his clan are the only black folks livin around here. You're sure this man is a Negro?" The mayor attempted to remain calm, but inside he was digesting the effect of having a black leader in El Chico.

"I met him yesterday," said Doug Farnsworth. "Him and his wife came by the truck stop. They are de-fi-nite-ly black and they have two big, tall high school boys; a good lookin family, if I do say so. The wife's already been hired by the county to teach history, computers, and girl's physical education at our high school. The boys are enrolling today and the Reverend starts preachin Sunday."

Ed Hawkins smiled with satisfaction. "It makes me proud to see El Chico bein a real progressive town. Y'all have to know the whole country is melting together race-wise and I guess this is El Chico's first big step to innergration."

Straightening his plaid bow tie Oliver Brumfeld screeched. "As I see it, the thing we have to think about is how our citizens will react. We don't want upheaval in town. We already have people on edge with our water problem and some are moving away, sellin out, and we're lookin like a ghost town. We cain't afford to lose more."

"Our tax base is dwindlin fast. I don't like it." Treasurer Herb Matson held up a computer spreadsheet with columns of numbers.

"Next thing you know we'll have slums and gangs and stuff." Oliver's eyes crossed behind his thick glasses. "It's a fact Negras bring down real estate values.

Bea McPherson sat in the back corner of the room taking notes surrounded by stacks of paperback books recently donated to the library. She typed as fast as she could in her new laptop computer.

"Gentlemen. Once again I am forced to interrupt this stupid, disgraceful discussion. I've had the pleasure of interviewing the new family and you can read my article on the front page of the *El Chico Times Gazette*. We are fortunate to have the Hansons choose to move to El Chico. Frankly, why they would is a mystery to me, other than they want their family to enjoy small town life." She stood up, packed her gear, and walked toward the door. "And, I will add, their degrees, experiences, and background put each of us to shame." She slammed the door on her way out.

The men were shocked into silence until the mayor spoke. "Well, council, I guess the die is cast and the ball is in play. Let's thank Lester for bringin us together for this special meetin. Time will tell what will happen with this new circumstance. All we can do is be supportive of our fair town. I know the council and the Methodists will behave well and will welcome this family with open arms. Won't you?" The mayor pounded his gavel and dismissed the group.

As soon as he could get privacy the mayor dialed his secret partner's private phone, reaching his voice mail. "I thought you'd like to know the Methodist Church just put us closer to our goal. There's a new minister in town along with his family, and they're niggers. I predict we'll have lots of property on the market within the next two weeks. Let me know if you're ready to move ahead with more acquisitions."

When Nick picked up the message he cussed and tossed the phone down hard on his desk. "Percy is more backward than I ever dreamed. The next time we're together I'll tell him that if he ever uses the N word again I'll knock him out!"

NEW PREACHER

The Reverend James Hanson and his wife had requested a small town with a school where their two sons could play football on an experienced team. They wanted to leave crowded city life but never expected to be sent to a practically all-white community. The minister knew this appointment was not going to be easy when he agreed to take the post.

"I simply cain't believe my eyes," Ethel Ogletree leaned towards her friend as she adjusted her bifocals.

"Yes, he is absolutely black, or at least dark brown." Minnie Lee Gibbons squinted attempting to improve her focus on the man sitting in a chair behind the podium.

"Hmmm. I never would have figured the Methodist Church bishops in Dallas would have sent a Negra here to El Chico," Ethel said.

Minnie whispered back. "Well, I heard he's *one of them*, those Dallas city people. In Bea's column I read he graduated from SMU's Theology School, top of his class."

"Wow." Ethel poked Minnie and pointed a finger. "And, look over there. That must be his family all lined up in the third row."

Clarajean lead the congregation in singing several selections from the hymnal accompanied by Mabel and Gertrude.

Then the new minister stepped to the podium. He smiled as he looked across the small congregation.

"Good morning, everyone." He continued smiling in spite of the cynical faces staring back at him. "I'm Reverend James Hanson and I have the pleasure of being appointed as your interim minister. I know my appearance may not be what you expected, but my wife,

Adelle, and our two sons, Jim Junior and Baines are very happy to join your community, even for a few months. Adelle and boys, please stand."

The congregation's heads turned in unison like observers in a tennis match straining to get a look at the family, the lovely, olive-skinned mom and the two over-six-feet tall boys. One by one the worshipers joined Bea McPherson in applause.

"Thank you for that warm welcome. I understand El Chico is struggling with many challenges, the foremost being a drought that is causing an economic crisis. I encourage each of you to pray for one another and for this community during these difficult times. I know I will. Remember, the Lord answers our prayers." He continued with a short sermon about droughts and hardships and answered prayers. He ended by saying, "My family looks forward to getting to know each of you personally. Feel free to call or come by the church office if you have questions, or if I can help you with any of your personal challenges. I trust the Lord God Almighty in His wisdom, knowing He knows what He is doing in all phases of our lives. Let's bow our heads in a word of prayer."

With that, the minister prayed what would later be referred to as a great and enlightened prayer. However, on that Sunday, only a few of the parishioners stopped to shake his hand on their way out the door.

DISCOVERY

Jake heard Bea's horse galloping through the chill of the early fall morning before he looked out his cabin door and saw her riding towards him.

"Bea, what's wrong?"

Bea slid from Starfire and tied her to what served as Jake's porch railing. She pulled some rolled up papers from her pack. "Don't get all upset. I've been ridin and thinkin and thought it was time we talked about some things."

The cowboy smiled, unable to hide how glad he was to have a conversation with this woman. "Yeah. I guess it's time we talked. Before you say a word, I want you to know how sorry I am that I acted like such an ass at the ... I had no right to hit that bas ...," Jake paused, correcting himself, "man. Bea, I never wanted to cause any harm to you."

"I know that, but damn, Jake, I've never seen you act like that, hittin someone you don't even know."

A figure appeared in Jake's doorway. "Howdy there, Bea. I was just leavin, wasn't I, Jake?"

"Please don't leave, Crow. This is perfect timing," said the woman. "Jake, you and I will have a long personal talk soon. There are some major issues we need to clear up between the two of us but they'll have to wait. Meanwhile, I need to talk to both of you about water, the pipeline, the tower, and something else."

The three sat inside Jake's cabin. The fire in the small iron stove kept the place warm and filled with the smell of coffee.

"Months ago, when we had the town meeting, Nick dropped some of his papers. I picked them up, intending to return them.

They've been in my storage closet under stacks of stuff. Until last night, when I was talking with Harold, I forgot all about the incident. I want y'all to look at these surveys. They don't look right to me." She spread the torn, dirty blueprints out on Jake's worn table.

Silver Crow spoke in his usual calm but decisive manner. "Bea, I don't have to look at these surveys. I know what they'll show. Before we go a word further, I need to tell you what I just finished telling Jake. It has everything to do with what you want to talk about and it might change what you have to say."

She nodded her head, poured all three coffees, each with a splash from Jake's bottle of Southern Comfort, and listened.

The chief continued, "From the first time H_2O Engineering's Graystone arrived in El Chico I sensed something evil. The man's presence was out of place. Part of what I'll tell you is absolute fact and part is my assessment of the situation."

"Jake, Crow, if this is gossip about Nick and me, then forget it. I only came for help deciding what these papers mean. I don't need any interference in my personal life from either of you." She began to roll the papers readying to leave.

"Bea, this ain't nothin about my own private reasons for not wantin Graystone to be around you. Once you hear what Crow has to say, you'll start questioning his motives. Don't go off getting all huffy before you know what's true." said Jake.

Silver Crow leaned back, took a gulp of coffee, and explained. "Serving on the board over in Austin gives me access to some insider information and, I'll admit, I had some friends do some nosin around about H_2O and its owner. Bottom line, Graystone is an out and out crook, should be in prison and here's why. His firm is nothing but an empty office at a fancy address with a good lookin administrative assistant. There are no engineers, other than Nick, who's not even a registered engineer. So first off, he misrepresented himself."

Bea sat down and gathered her emotions. "Nick took me to his office when I was in Dallas and I met Jaynell, his assistant. She was very nice and he explained the vacant offices saying all the other employees were out in the field working. So you're tellin me his office was all fake?"

"There's been an ongoing official investigation of Graystone and his firm for the past two years, but the law hasn't been able to find any proof of illegal activities so far. I understand they've traced corporate moneys from several suspicious sources back to his personal accounts in Dallas. Among those funds is a check written to H_2O by the town of El Chico. By the way, the big home is a rental and he leases the Lexus."

"But, but," She stuttered, "when I went to Dallas Nick was such a great host, and such a gentleman."

Jake frowned. "He damn well better 'ave been a gentleman."

"You've got nerve. What right do you have to judge who is or isn't a gentleman!" Bea scowled back at him.

Jake continued. "Sorry to say, but there's more and it's very distressing so I'm glad you're sitting down. Graystone and Percy, along with Etta Ruth, have been meetin and talkin on the phone regularly for the past year, long before Graystone and Percy started this pipeline talk here in El Chico. There's no firm evidence they're involved in anything together that's against the law, but it appears that way."

Silver Crow added. "It's a fact that Percy and Graystone have formed a real estate investment corporation and have purchased or are in the process of purchasing numerous properties in El Chico. Most are on the east side, in the area around the base of the mountain. Etta Ruth's family property is mortgaged to the hilt and Percy has been taking funds out of their bank accounts like a crazy man."

Bea's eyes grew big. "Maybe they're trying to save El Chico by investing here."

Jake shook his head and continued the story. "The mayor hasn't told anyone about his partnership with Graystone. Not disclosing their relationship is illegal, plain and simple. Crow and I think once they own the majority of land on the east side, they plan to build some kind of project because we've seen surveyors marking out something. Maybe they're just designing lots to sell off."

"If they're building something then that's good for El Chico, right?"

"No, Bea, not if they're frightening people out of El Chico to buy their property cheap and then profiting from the deception." Jake slapped the table with his hand. "We've wondered if they had anything to do with the fire or the robberies."

The three sat together drinking and discussing the possibilities. Bea made a list of the facts they knew for sure.

"I think I know part of his plan." Tears formed in the corners of Bea's eyes. She told about Nick's idea for making the Circle McP into a dude ranch.

"Damn it to hell!" Jake stood up and paced. "A dude ranch? I'd hit him again if he was here."

"He told me the town is goin to die even with the pipeline and I'll have to shut down the cattle business sometime soon. He made so much sense when he talked to me."

"What a low-life bastard!" Jake emptied his cup and filled it up again, more liquor than coffee.

"That's not the worse thing, Bea." Silver Crow interrupted, "The reason I don't have to see these papers is that we know Graystone's assessment of the water level at the mountain aquifer was bogus. The actual level is much higher than he's told the council. Graystone knew the accurate amounts from the beginning. From the looks of things he deliberately falsified reports."

"You mean he out and out lied to the town and to me? The pipeline project is nothin but a scam? Damn it to hell! Bea stood and paced the floor. "All along I didn't like the sound of it. When I saw these papers I thought something didn't look right. Still, it's so hard to believe. Oh my God. I feel like such a dummy."

Tears spilled down Bea's face. "I just can't believe Nick planned to swindle El Chico from the beginning, or that Etta Ruth would stoop to something so dishonest and cruel. As difficult as she is, she loves this town. And Percy … well it's easier to believe he might do something shady, but this, this is just too horrible." She sat covering her face with her hands.

"Bea, I'm so sorry." Jake leaned over and put his hand on her shoulder. "Here. Take a big swallow. I've never seen you so upset." He poured more liquor into her cup and handed it to her. Jake used a consoling tone. "We don't know for certain Percy and Etta knew about the true water level but we're gonna find out."

A determined, angry expression replaced Bea's tears. "I've never been so mad in all my life. I think the three of us know there's an illegal scheme goin on to cheat El Chico's citizens, including yours truly. We have to find out everything we can and get proof for the authorities." The three friends continued to think, drink, and plan, until the sun dropped below the flat prairie.

THE PLAN

Sunday the church's pews were dotted with attendees, mostly curious members who had to see the black man in the flesh to believe the rumors. Bea sat up front and listened as the new minister gave a moving sermon. "I have talked with a number of you and understand how critical the water shortage is and what a burden you have to carry each day, fearing the worst. The situation reminds me of many Biblical examples of people struggling, of famines and droughts. Throughout the scriptures we are given God's promise that He is watching over us and that He has a plan for each of our lives. I will close with passages of great hope from Psalm 104. These words seem to be written just for El Chico. 'He sends forth springs in the valleys. They flow between the mountains. They give drink to every beast of the field. He causes the grass to grow for the cattle. The earth is satisfied with the fruit of His works.'" Once again he ended with a prayer that even the most skeptical attendees found impressive.

"I'm tellin you, this preacher has a gift, straight from God. Even if he is Negra, he is for sure an important messenger. You have to come to church next week." Ethel Ogletree repeated this message over and over to friends.

The next Sunday every Methodist in town returned to church and even a few of the Baptists visited just to hear what the new preacher had to say.

"Reverend Hanson, thanks for seeing me again." Bea sat across from the minister in his small office. He was unloading boxes filled with books, putting them into shelves.

"Anytime Bea, and please call me James. You're my first official visitor. I appreciate the nice article you wrote about my family in the Gazette." James Hanson smiled.

"I believe you'll find folks here to be good, honest, and friendly. Many have spent their entire lives right here and don't care much about what's happening in the rest of the country, much less the world. When a few of our young people joined the military and were sent to the mideast, they became more interested. Until recently, most didn't know where Afghanistan was and they sure didn't understand why we'd fight over there."

"I'm not sure anyone really knows the answer to that question."

"Anyway, you'll have the congregation packing the church every Sunday in short time. I'll do all I can to help your family get settled."

"I thank you. Adelle and I will do fine but we're concerned about our boys. We'll let you know if we need help on their account. Now, Bea, what can I do for you today?"

"Reverend Hanson, I mean, James, you know that El Chico won't exist much longer without water. We need rain desperately."

"Yes, I've been reading back copies of the papers so I think I'm pretty up–to-date with the pipeline debate and the tower project."

'There's more,' said Bea. "We've been told by one company, the one that wants to put in a pipeline, the aquifer is completely dry. A few of us question the report's source. This is off the record, but I want you to know, I'm hiring an independent surveyor to reassess the area out by the mountain at the gap. That's behind the motel where the tower is located. Counting you, only five of us know what I'm doing. If there's water we might also find some illegal activities."

"Well, that sounds intriguing. If you get a good report, this might be the answer to the town's drought problems. Thank you for alerting me about the possible trouble. People need a good relationship with God when there's trouble."

"You're right about that. But, we need more help from you."

"More?"

"Yes. Regardless, of the aquifer level, we need rain. I don't know how you'll feel about this, but here it is, and I hope you'll give it some serious consideration."

Bea shared her idea of a joint ceremony between Silver Crow's Native Americans and the church, mapping out details for the new minister.

"You'll be an important part of this." She concluded her proposition volunteering to write a special section in the *El Chico Tribune and Gazette* about the Methodists. It would appear each week, free of charge.

The reverend shook Bea's hand as she left the church. "Bea, I'll pray about your request, listen for the Lord's guidance and then I'll let you know my decision."

Three days later Reverend Hanson called Bea accepting the idea of the joint ceremony and the ongoing news reports about the church.

☆ ☆ ☆

"All along I didn't trust that snake-in-the-grass Graystone." Ed sat with Jake and Bea in his salvage yard office waiting for the surveyor to arrive. "By God, I'm on board with y'all, one-hundred and ten percent. We have to do all we can to expose that Dallas scoundrel for trying to exploitate our fine town."

☆ ☆ ☆

"Thanks for drivin all the way over." Ed introduced his long-time friend, Gavin Atherson, to the group. "Gavin's head of Lone Star Engineering and Geology. We used to play some football against each other years ago."

Gavin patted Ed on the back, a big grin across his face. "This ol boy's the one who made me give up the game. I remember like it was yesterday: our big playoff game, colder than Alaska, ground hard as bricks and your tackle laid me flat on my back. I wanted no more after that. I switched to drag racin." The two laughed as the engineer spread charts across Ed's desk. "It's just as you thought, the graphs you were shown last spring weren't accurate. In fact, we have no idea what your guy meant by showin you these because they aren't from anywhere in Texas."

"Yeah, that's what we figured, not El Chico," said Jake.

"Let's look at El Chico's survey. You can see the underground water flow here, here, and there," said Gavin, pointing to the points on his drawings. "It's true the aquifer is lower than the state's last reading ten years ago, but we think there's enough water to supply El Chico for years to come, if you'll follow current water-saving trends and if it ever rains again regular."

"That's great news for our town. Thanks, Gav," said Ed slapping his friend on the back.

"How about gettin it out of the ground?" Jake scratched his head.

"You'll have to go deep, but the water is there. There is one potential problem that could be serious."

"That's all we need, a serious problem," said Ed.

"This area still has a large concentration of silica along with gypsum. Before drilling you need to know our geologists say there are some areas of anhydrite, which could be highly explosive. It's unusual but if certain conditions including extreme pressure occur, we believe deep underground energy releases would cause the ground to shift. There's evidence that's what caused this unusual mountain formation several million years ago."

"Man oh man, who would ever've thought we had a bomb sittin under the mountain!" Ed paced the floor.

"Now Ed, you don't need to go worrying about this. We still recommend drilling. The mountain has been sittin there most of forever and everything has been fine. I'm just sayin it's a good idea to be aware of this during your recovery process."

Ed, Jake, and Bea went over the charts again asking every question they thought Silver Crow might want to know. They wrote names and details about drilling companies, placing the information in a secure metal case Ed bought at the airline lost luggage sale.

Gavin picked up a large box filled with chrome and made his way out the door. "By the way, Ed, thanks for the trade. I've been havin a heck of a time findin matching hubcaps for my Mustang and the gas cap, well, it's impossible to find an original like this one."

Ed smiled at his circle of friends. "Gavin has the prettiest '71 fastback you'd ever want to see." Slapping the surveyor on his back again, Ed continued, "Gav, I was happy I could help you and at the same time help us."

As the engineer drove away, Jake guffawed. "Ed, you beat all. Do you ever pay real money for anything?"

"Not if I can hep it. Just glad I had what he wanted."

"Now we have proof Graystone gave the town a false report." Bea smiled her most satisfied smile.

That evening Bea called Nick according to plan. "Hi, there. It's Bea." She hoped her voice was upbeat and positive, not showing her anger. She'd like to kick him where it would hurt most, but uncovering his dishonesty was more important.

"What a great surprise." The big man turned off his television and smiled. It was good to hear her voice again.

"I'll get right to the point, Nick. I've been thinking about your idea for the dude ranch and I'm considering it. While I just hate the thought of a bunch of city slickers roaming around my property, maybe it's something I have to do. I'd appreciate your ideas on how to put the project together."

"What do you want to know? I'm ready right now to share my concept of an El Chico ranch designed for tourism. I've done research using some very successful ranches in Colorado and Montana as my models."

"I mean in person. When will you be out this way again? We could get together and really discuss this. I'd like for you to spend a couple of days lookin around the Circle McP. I can show you how the ranch works now. Maybe you can share specific thoughts how it might convert to a dude resort."

"I can clear my calendar and get out there in three days if that's okay with you." *It's time for me to get another check from Percy, anyway. This will be perfect.*

"Okay. Wednesday it is. I have a big guest room here at my house, so it will be real convenient."

"I'll call you when I'm on my way." The man hung up and clapped his hands together. *A room at her house.* This is good news.

Bea hung up the phone and cheered. Jake was standing by her. He reached over and gave her a big hug. "Well done, Bea. Well done. Of course I'll be hangin close by since that two-faced SOB will be stayin in your house."

Bea returned the hug. "Thanks, Jake, for always being there for me."

He looked at her and their eyes locked. "Bea, I am so sorry. Sorry for what you've been through and, for, well everything." He held her in the closest embrace they'd ever shared. Bea's heart beat in perfect time with his. "I guess I'd better go." He turned around and walked out the door.

"Damn him!" she said to herself. Bea's eyes filled with tears for the second time in years. "Men! To hell with them."

✷ ✷ ✷

Bea called Ed and Silver Crow to tell them another step of the plan was in place.

Silver Crow was in Austin meeting with state water board hydrologists to get the state's latest survey of the trans-Pecos area aquifer. Jake, back in El Chico, played detective following the mayor wherever he went. Meanwhile, Ed pursued information about drilling for water at the El Chico site.

Next, Bea called her brother so the two could bring each other up to date. The private detective Harold hired confirmed that Nicholas Graystone was an opportunist skirting the edge of the law. "Bea, he is not someone you want to fool with. Violent acts, like El Chico's recent fire and robberies, seem to follow him like a plague. Be careful. Graystone could be dangerous."

DUDE VISITS THE RANCH

Bea greeted her guest at the front door. He was wearing a dark brown western suit with beige trim and shirt and another pair of custom boots. These had a longhorn head and horns plastered on the toe, wrapping around and up the sides.

"Hi there. It's good to see you, Nick."

He frowned at the cats that roamed the porch, but smiled at Bea, leaning in to give her a hug. She turned away leading him into the large vaulted living room.

"Bea, this is charming. I had no idea your house was so large. That antler chandelier is really something. I don't think I've ever seen one like it."

"Yes, my daddy made it himself. In fact he built the house." She pointed to a sitting area surrounding an enormous rock fireplace. "Have a seat. I made some Sangria and a few snacks, thinking you'd be hungry."

The man continued to scan the room. He walked from one area to another before sitting in the appointed cowhide chair. "You continue to amaze me, Bea. I'm glad you're considering the dude ranch idea. Your place is perfect for such a project. I can just picture couples sitting around this fireplace with glasses of wine."

Bea turned her head and grimaced, then turned back towards Graystone and smiled.

After small talk over the snacks, Bea led Nick to a large guest room. "Put your bags down and come with me so I can show you around the rest of the house. Once we're through here, Jake and I'll take you around the property."

"Jake! He doesn't seem to like me and I'd sure hate to get in a confrontation with him again."

"No worries there! Jake was just being protective. He's like that to anyone new in my life. I'll be honest, his initial reaction to the dude ranch idea was as bad as mine but when we discussed the water shortage and the town's decline and probable demise, he wanted to learn more, just like I do. I'm always interested in a money-making endeavor."

"If you're sure, Bea. I don't want any trouble with Jake."

"We'll make a day of it, stay out until dusk; have dinner around a campfire. 'Campfire Dinners' is one of the ideas I have for possible dude ranch entertainment."

For the next hour Bea showed Nick the house, the barn, the land around the main complex. Pointing to what was left of the once-flowing spring Bea asked, "So, Nick, you think the aquifer is about gone?"

Casting his eyes downward the man looked sad. "Yes, Bea. I'm afraid so. That's why the pipeline is a must."

Bea deliberately guided the man into the chicken pen where his fancy boots couldn't avoid the combination of feed and shit. She watched as he stepped over the rocky terrain dodging aggressive chickens. "We used to have ducks but they went away when our pond got so dry."

"Oh, I see." He stomped his feet trying to rid the prized boots of debris.

Bea turned her head so the man wouldn't see her wide grin. "Oh, here comes Jake now." She eyed the sunny horizon looking at the dust cloud marking Jake's truck and horse trailer. "Nick, I think you might want to change into some jeans and more work-style clothes for the ride."

"What ride?"

"You do ride, don't you?" Bea tilted her head looking up at the man.

"Oh, sure."

"Well, Jake's bringing you a horse so you can see every part of the ranch. You can get a real feel for what a McP dude ranch might be like."

"Oh, okay, that sounds fine. I haven't ridden for years but it's like a bike, right? Once you can ride you never forget." He smiled and followed her back to the house in time to meet Jake. Buster and Sam barked, running full force towards Nick after they scrambled out of the truck's cab. The man's body stiffened and his eyes grew large as the big dogs approached.

"Hey boys. Settle down." Jake's voice boomed. "This here's Bea's friend." The dogs ran around the stranger a few times then bounded to Bea. She scratched and petted them.

"Good dogs. Good dogs." Nick's voice shook as he attempted to make friends. Taking the man's words as an invitation, Buster jumped up putting his dirty paws on Nick's chest while he licked his face. Not expecting the weight of the animal, Nick staggered backwards, catching a boot on a rock. He fell into a muddy rivulet that was once a part of the stream feeding the house's pond. His beige, ten-gallon hat floated through the air and landed in the middle of the sludge.

"Oh no!" Bea hid her amusement with looks of horror. "I'm so sorry, Nick. Down Buster! Jake, please call the dogs."

Nick struggled up, wiping mud and dirt off. The more he wiped the dirtier he looked. "It's okay. I should've watched myself. I don't see a need to change into jeans now." He managed to laugh. "Having wild ranch animals around is something we city people aren't used to."

Jake handed him his filthy hat. "Yep. That's probably one of them things you'll have to talk to us about. If we're gonna have city folks stayin on the ranch we'll have to make sure it's safe for them. Of course, I figure they'll like getting a real ranch experience." Jake leaned against the truck and grinned. "I'd better get the horses unloaded so we can get started."

"Jake, I made some sandwiches for you to take along." Bea ran back to the house and returned with a bag.

"Bea, aren't you going with us? I thought you would show me around with Jake."

"I'll meet you at Jake's cabin around four, in time to get ready for our campfire supper."

Jake prepared the horses, and loaded additional supplies. He motioned for Nick to join him. "You do know how to ride, don't ya?"

"It's been awhile but I'll do fine." Jake held the reins while Nick got on the large animal. He jerked when the horse snorted and shook his mane.

"This here's Tornado."

"Tornado! Why's he called Tornado?"

"He's well-trained but sometimes gets a bit feisty, goes around in circles if he thinks his rider is doubtful. So, Graystone, act like you know what you're doin and you'll be fine. All you have to do is follow me."

Nick waved to Bea as Tornado trailed Jake and Pearce into the distance.

Bea turned back to the house and doubled over laughing when she reached the safety of the porch. "I hope Jake doesn't kill the man. We need him alive."

✯ ✯ ✯

For more than an hour the twosome rode back and forth across the ranch prairie as Jake pointed out dried arroyos, dead brush, and rock formations. As they reached a slight rise covered by mesquite and scrub oak, he explained to Nick that this part of the ranch had historic significance. "The early natives had a burial ground and did some ceremonial stuff around here. Maybe this would be interesting to dudes."

"Oh yeah. Everyone would be interested in Indian history and stuff like that." Nick squirmed in his saddle, his backside feeling a little tender.

"Let's do a little explorin," said Jake, dismounting.

Nick stayed on his horse not sure how to get off the tall animal. Seeing his problem, Jake walked over and held the reins while the visitor slid off. "Nick, I don't want to tell you what to do, but it's wise to always mount and dismount on the left side of a horse. Also, be real sure your boot heels are clear from both stirrups before starting to get off. If not, you could get caught, dragged, and hurt real bad."

"Oh, I knew that. Just forgot." Nick looked tired. Jake tied both horses to a tree and walked down a trail with Nick following. As Jake rounded a grove of junipers he jumped back, drew his pistol and fired several times, yelling, "Oh my God! Rattlers, rattlers!" Nick jumped three feet into the air.

Jake had a hard time holding his laughter as he watched the large man in his filthy clothes dance around in fear. Several large dead snakes lay in the rocks where Jake had aimed his pistol. "They're all over the place here. Do you think rattlers'll be a problem for dudes?"

Once the man calmed down he answered. "Jake, I wouldn't want to surprise anyone with lethal snakes, and the liability could be great. Rattlers would be a problem for paying customers on a dude ranch." Nick continued following the cowboy looking right and left in panic mode. "Don't you think this is enough Indian stuff?"

"We haven't even come to a mound yet," Jake pointed. "There's one about twenty feet away. The natives camped in this area for centuries and there're all kinds of artifacts just lying around. You might even find an arrowhead to take back to Dallas with you."

"You don't mean it? A real one?"

For the next half hour Jake stood in the shade of a small oak tree while he watched Nick look through a pile of rocks with the afternoon sun offering its full force of rays. Nick's jacket had long since been stored in a saddlebag and his shirttail was hanging over his pants. "I think that's enough now, Nick. Let's have a bite of the sandwiches Bea made and then head back to my place. I'll take you by what's left of the cattle herd on our way."

Nick stumbled across the rocky trail, pockets full of rocks, watching out for more snakes. After gobbling the food, Jake helped Nick back onto Tornado and they headed off to the back pasture. "Up ahead you'll see Duke Five and the three cows we have left."

"They look pretty out there eating grass."

"That's hay they're eatin because most of the grass is dead."

As the two men made their way close to the almost dry pond, the livestock saw Jake and headed towards him.

Nick's muscles tightened. "They're gonna charge us, Jake. What'll we do?"

"First of all, they aren't chargin and second, be calm. No animals, cow or horse, like nervous humans. You'll let off a scent that scares them."

"Okay. Okay. I'll try, but these are really big cows."

Jake pulled up to the well at the side of the pond and dismounted. Nick followed, still saddled up. Jake checked the water level and remounted. "Do you think dudes will like visitin with the cows?"

"Well, I'm not sure but I guess so," said a visibly shaky Nick.

"It's time we head to my place, where Bea will meet us," said Jake turning Pearce around.

When Tornado saw Jake's horse turn towards home, he knew they were heading back to his source of food and water. He whinnied, raised his head, spun around and without hesitation went into a full gallop.

"Nick. Nick. Pull back on the reins!" Jake yelled as loud as he could. "Head down! Hold on!"

Nick knew enough to hold the reins and grab the saddle horn. His legs flapped wildly against the horse's flanks and the man screamed at the top of his voice, "Help! Heeeeellllllp!" The animal interpreted the yelling as encouragement to go even faster.

Jake followed close behind to be sure Tornado was taking the direct trail. *Serves the sorry devil right for being such a liar and cheat.* Jake was laughing so hard that he could barely hold on to Pearce's reins.

Bea met Nick and the runaway horse at Jake's cabin where Tornado stopped, ready to eat. All the blood had drained from Nick's face and he was as still as a statue, frozen in place on the horse's back.

"What happened, Nick? You sure were ridin back fast. Guess you like speed from back in your Dallas Cowboy football days?" Bea patted the horse's flank.

When the man could catch his breath he sighed, "No, Bea. This horse went fast all on his own and I couldn't slow him down."

"Oh. Sorry, Nick. I'm sure Jake thought you'd realize when a horse knows it's time to go home and eat they like to get there as fast as their rider lets them. It's a horse thing."

"No. Jake didn't warn me about that."

"Well, get down and help me get the gear off. Jake can take care of the rest for you." Nick was covered with brush scratches, dirt and mud. His boots were unrecognizable, hat missing and face sunburned to a crisp.

"Bea, I think I'll skip dinner.

"Oh Nick, I know you'll like the campfire and meal. Right now you need a strong drink. Come on and have a seat out here under the scrub oaks where there's a breeze. I'm anxious to hear more of your ideas about the Circle McP Dude Ranch."

For the next hour the threesome relaxed. Jake made a small fire, roasted strips of steak and potatoes on sticks and they watched the sun setting in the distance. At dusk they heard a shrill sound.

"Now what was that?" The Dallas man jerked out of his relaxed mood.

"Oh, that was a coyote. They're all around but we won't see them. But they see us." Jake leaned back and took a sip out of a flask. "You ever hear the Comanche legend of the coyote?"

"No. I don't know much Indian lore, but maybe that would be a good thing for your future guests to enjoy; campfire stories told by a real cowboy like you, Jake."

"Nope. I'm not gonna be the one to tell sacred tales." Jake frowned at Nick.

"Nick, that's a good idea," said Bea. " Jake, go ahead and tell the story. You can leave out anything sacred."

"Well, okay. The story goes somethin' like this. Once there was a Comanche warrior who wanted to gain respect from his fellow warriors by being the most fearsome hero in the bunch. But he didn't get even one scalp or buffalo hide or whatever on a raid, so, he lied about his conquests, something forbidden by the Comanche nation. His tribe paid tribute to him and he wore the feathers of a leader. Somehow the coyotes knew he was not a true warrior so every night they haunted him, howling and howling, keeping him from sleep until he went completely mad and ran screaming into the wilderness. The natives say the lying warrior's soul is still roaming this part of Texas followed by a pack of animals. Of course the native version is long and detailed and scary as hell."

"That's quite a story all right." Nick's eyes were wide as he looked over the prairie and up to the mountain. The last remnants of the sunset had faded fast. As if on clue, coyotes began howling, the campfire died and the moon went behind some clouds, transforming the camp into a shadowed, haunted place. "I think we should head back to your house, Bea. I've seen the ranch and think you have plenty to work with to make the Circle McP into a fine dude resort."

"I can drive you to the main house and Jake'll take care of the horses. My car is parked over there." Bea pointed into the dark. "Just follow me." She walked away from Nick and he followed but lost sight of her. "Bea. Bea. Where are you? I can't see a thing."

"She's right over there." Jake's voice came from another place in the dark.

"I'm telling you, I can't see a thing."

"I'm just over here." Bea's voice seemed far away. Nick hurried in that direction.

"Keep talking, Bea. I'm lost and still can't tell where you are."

"You're okay. Just keep walking."

Bea's voice seemed to have moved behind him so he turned around. The man stumbled and fell over some rocks. He heard a rustling sound and then the sound of a coyote no more than ten yards away. "Help, Bea! Jake! There's a coyote over here and it might attack." There was silence for what seemed like minutes and more coyote howling and rustling. Then a shrill scream permeated the area and more rustling and howling. "Help! Help!" Nick yelled over and over.

Then someone grabbed him from behind. "I guess you got turned around, Nick. That's easy to do when you ain't used to complete dark like we get out on the prairie." Regardless of Nick's dislike of the cowboy, Jake's presence was reassuring. "The coyotes are gone. I ain't never heard of them attackin a human unless they're starving." He guided Nick to Bea's car, where she was waiting with the engine running.

Once Jake had Nick inside the car Bea drove over the bumpy road back to the main ranch house. "I hope you had fun seein the ranch, Nick, in spite of the dirt and such. I know it's a bit strange to a city man like yourself but it is beautiful in its own way."

"Bea, I admit I was way out of my comfort zone being here but I do think you have something special that could be of commercial value. I'm just too tired to think about it right now." Nick pulled himself out of the Escalade and forced his body up the steps to the house. He went right to the guest room and shut the door. There would be no romancing Bea tonight.

Just as Nick's eyes closed he heard a coyote's howl. It seemed to be right outside his window. He put a pillow over his head and dozed. All though the night, he heard the band of animals howling and other creatures screaming. It was worse than any nightmare he'd ever had.

At 8:00 a.m., Bea was in the kitchen, ready with a full ranch style breakfast. The smell of bacon and coffee filtered into Nick's room and he forced his aching body to shower. *I've never been so ready to get away from a place in my life.* He looked in the mirror at his bright red face.

After eating and drinking several cups of coffee, Nick looked at his hostess thinking once again how attractive she was. "Thanks so much, Bea, for your hospitality and the tour. You are an amazing woman. I apologize, but, I've got to get back to Dallas right away for a big business conference."

"Nick, I'm so disappointed you won't be stayin longer. There's much more to do on the Circle McP. And, you said once you toured the property we were going to discuss ideas you have for the dude ranch."

"Bea, it's like I thought, you'll have the perfect spot for a world class dude resort when you have regular water. I don't think I need to see more to know that."

"But, Nick, I was looking forward to taking you up to the top of the mountain to show you the old Comanche burial ground and the construction site for the water tower. That's the area where the remains of the old lake and main spring are. I know you'll want to see that."

"Yes. I do want to see everything and I'll be back soon. The mayor invited me to come to the water tower dedication."

Bea watched as the sunburned, bruised, and humiliated man drove down the road and turned north on the highway. "I can only hope the sounds of coyotes kept him up all night and that he dreams about them when he gets back to Dallas," she said turning to Jake and Silver Crow.

"We did the best we could howling and screaming all night. We're the ones who didn't get any sleep." Silver Crow grinned and sat on the porch steps, Buster and Sam joining him.

"I liked the rattlesnake sighting. Crow, those old snake carcasses did the trick. The man didn't make a move without checking all around to be sure he wasn't stepping on a snake."

The trio laughed until their sides ached.

THE CEREMONY

Bea waited for Etta Ruth to get settled before making her entrance, wanting the mayor's wife to hear all of what she would say. She entered the Cut 'n Curl in an excited burst. "Hi everyone. I have exciting personal news."

Every woman in the salon stopped what she was doing. This was out of character for Bea. She never shared her personal news.

"First of all, we're goin to have an extra ceremony at the Water Tower Dedication next Thursday evening at 6:00. I know some of you don't approve, but I'm sure you will want to be a part of this. Both Silver Crow and Reverend Hanson will lead a prayer service asking for rain. It's joint church and Native American. After the Mayor does the dedication, the ceremony will begin. Please pass the word along. This is real special."

Minnie Lee and Marjorie frowned but Bea continued. "And, Nick Graystone visited the Circle McP this week." Bea was pleased with the shocked looks. "He is very interested in partnering with me and making the Circle McP into a hotel and dude ranch. He thinks we could be the future star industry for El Chico; that it could turn the entire town's economy around."

Etta Ruth's mouth dropped open so wide half a donut fell into her lap. "Why, I didn't know Nick was here this week."

"Why would you know, Etta?" Lulu Belle turned to look at the pudgy woman with spiked gobs of raven dye in her hair.

"Everyone knows Nick and the mayor are good friends. They are working on the pipeline together." Etta looked around at the other ladies to be sure they understood her position.

"Oh that," said Bea stroking her red curls as she looked in the mirror. "Nick said we might not have to have the pipeline if we drill for water on the Circle McP. He has the best ideas and I'm seriously considering his offer to invest in my project. He would put in a large amount to get it started. It's time I took it a little easy plus I could spend part of my time visiting Nick in Dallas."

"Well, I never heard of such a thing," Etta Ruth was stunned.

"This is a big surprise, but a good one," added Lulu Belle. "It could be wonderful for you and for El Chico."

"Well, I have to run along but I just had to share this wonderful news with all of you. Remember next Thursday at 6:00 for the big celebration and ceremony." Bea turned around and raced out the door and across the street where she hid to see just how fast Etta Ruth could get her hair fixed and make her way to Percy.

☆ ☆ ☆

All week the town looked forward to the event advertised as the "Dedication of the Tower and Group Prayer for Rain." The only people not attending were the few die-hard Christians who still fought the inclusion of Silver Crow and the Native Americans.

On the day of the ceremony, before sunrise, Silver Crow and Jake arrived at the apex of the mountain. After dismounting, the two men walked the secret paths around the native ceremonial ground as they watched the sun peek over the valley below. For hours both sat still and speechless, meditating about the land, its history and the power of nature, just as they had when they were young.

Mid morning they prepared the site for the evening's ceremony, then they returned to the ranch, riding slowly side by side.

"This is some idea Bea had and now it's happening." Jake pulled his hat low to protect himself from the sun.

"The People relied on ceremonies. Several bands met once a year. Sometimes thousands of people gathered. They'd trade, have a festival, and then a prayer session to address whatever crisis was at hand, like weather. Rain, or lack of it, determined if they'd live or not, just like it does now for El Chico."

"I'd like to believe your ceremony is going to make a difference but it's hard to think it will still work in modern times," said Jake.

"Prayer is basic human instinct. Since the beginning of time man has meditated and talked to the great creator. More often than not requests are answered. One thing for sure, rain or no rain we're gonna run Graystone out of town and the mayor is goin to have to fess up to his lying."

Jake chuckled. "I don't think we'll have any more problems with the Dallas cowboy after his dude ranch visit. I can't wait to see Percy. Bea says he's been havin nightmares for months about the mountain, so this evening should get him good."

Etta Ruth looked in her full-length mirror preparing for the ceremony. "Percy, you wouldn't believe what that Bea said to all the girls at the Cut 'n Curl. She said Nick and she are going into the dude ranch business and he's financing the whole thing, Can you believe that! Here we are puttin all our funds into the resort and he goes off and does this. Right now I just hate her and that man."

"Oh, Etta Ruth, Nick already told us he is tryin to buy her ranch. This is just his way of stringin her along. You just wait and see."

"Do you really think so?" Etta thought for a few moments and then smiled. "I guess Nick is smart enough not to let her take advantage of him. I'd like to see her drive her Escalade into the sunset and never return to El Chico."

"Etta, why did we have to agree to having this damn ceremony at the gap? I told you over and over how my nightmares are too real for me to be comfortable out there."

"Oh, honey-pie. You've faced worse things than this all your life. Remember when you asked Daddy for my hand?" Etta giggled and kissed the man's cheek as she tightened his bolo tie. "Besides, Nick is going to be there and we have to be sure he isn't dumping our project for Bea's dude ranch idea."

Percy's face turned red and expanded making him look like a

blowfish with a large mustache. "Etta Ruth, Nick has no intention of going into business with Bea, other than maybe monkey business." He laughed. Etta did not.

"I don't know what he sees in that cheap-lookin hussy."

"Sweetums, I'm not gonna say this again. Nick is trying to get her to sell the Circle McP to us so we can have it for the resort. That is all. She has no clue about his motives."

"I guess you're right, since you talk to him almost everyday. At any rate, we have to go to the ceremony. This is about as close to a kick-off for the resort as we'll have until we announce it formally."

While the first couple of El Chico was readying for the big event, Nick Graystone was making his way down the highway towards the small town. Nick hadn't slept through a night since he visited the Circle McP. Lack of sleep and dreams of howling coyotes haunted him making him fear he was going crazy. He would admit it to no one, almost didn't acknowledge it to himself, but the tale about the lying warrior crossed his mind several times a day.

"There couldn't be a grain of fact in some old Indian story. Besides I don't lie so much as I just don't tell the full truth." He talked to himself. "And everybody does that if they want to make the big bucks."

Nick was ready to move on to whatever was next in his life.

Thoughts of Bea flickered across his mind and he caught himself swerving off the road. *She's the spunkiest, smartest, sexiest woman I've met in years, but I've got to forget her. There's no way I'd ever live on a ranch and there's no way she's converting to being a city-girl.* At the onset of tears, he turned his CD player up so George Strait would drown out his thoughts. "All my exes live in Tex-as. Texas is the place I really long to beeeeee." Nick sang along.

The two friends met behind the motel an hour before the crowd arrived. Silver Crow had changed into his Comanche chief outfit, the one he wore when the press wanted to interview him about his ancestors and Comanche history.

"You look the part, like some kind of movie star," said Jake as he helped with the last preparations.

"Jake, you understand when to light the fires. Just after I finish my chant."

"Yeah. We've been over this enough. I agree, the fires will be quite a spectacle, especially with all the chemicals you added for color and smoke."

The chief looked up. "The funny thing is the sky already looks like rain. There's cloud cover from Dallas to Amarillo with some light showers and lots of lightning in that area. The weathermen say to expect rain in Fort Worth. But, we both know that's happened before and we don't get a drop here."

"This time you and the new Methodist preacher will be doin all you know how to do to change that." Jake pointed to a white van covered with Native American drawings. "I think I see your people."

"Yep. Come on and say hello."

Jake followed Crow for handshaking with costumed men and women.

Bea arrived with Ed and Odelia. The preacher and his family were close behind. By six o'clock the area around the motel, at the mountain's base, was packed with El Chico's citizens. A country carnival atmosphere prevailed. The church ladies passed out tiny flashlights to the crowd. Ed bought them at a liquidation sale years ago and thought they'd be a perfect complement to the ceremony.

"Bea, Bea." Nick called to her as he made his way through the crowd. This time he wore a black western suit with white piping. His boots were ink black covered with white Texas stars. "I made it, just like I promised I would."

"Oh, Nick. I'm so glad you found me. I have something for you." She motioned for him to follow her. She opened the back of her car and handed the roll of papers to the man. "I meant to give these to you when you visited the ranch so we could discuss them, but you left so quickly I didn't get to."

"What's this?"

"You dropped the drawings at the town meeting back when you told all of us about the water shortage and presented the pipeline idea. It's your schematic of what is supposed to be the water aquifer and springs in this area."

The man looked shocked. "I didn't miss these, but thank you just the same."

"No, thank you. I only picked them up so I could return them to you then I forgot all about it until after our visit in Dallas. When I looked the drawings over I realized they didn't make sense. But, you knew that all along. I kept waiting for you to tell me the truth but you haven't, Nick."

"Bea, let me explain." Nick's smile faded to concern.

"I know there's still water below the mountain, in fact, below us right now. How you live with yourself, I'll never know." Bea raised her voice. "Look around at these people. They are good souls and you've been out to cheat them. You tried to take their hard earned money, to say nothing of what you wanted to do to me. If I was a man I'd beat you to a pulp." With that she turned away and then turned back. "And, if you had anything to do with that prairie fire or the robbery at Lulu's I'll find out and do my best to have you put in jail." She walked away and turned around again and almost screamed. "And, it would be a cold day in hell when I'd partner with you to do anything." With an audible huff she walked away, not looking back to see the forlorn look and sunken shoulders of the Dallas businessman.

✯ ✯ ✯

"Ladies and gentlemen, welcome to the El Chico Water Tower Dedication and Rain Ceremony." Mayor Foremost spoke through a megaphone. His face was red and his body was soaked in cold sweat. He was anxious to exit the area. "Without further ado, I hand the program over to the El Chico Methodist Church's minister, Brother James Hanson."

Taking the megaphone from the mayor, the preacher began speaking. "Good evening. Let us begin with a word of prayer. Dear Heavenly Father, we come to you this evening recognizing your great power and love. We praise you, the provider of shelter and sustenance, for your creation, this beautiful earth, our home. Thank you for the gifts you give us each day. We come to you with this special service asking you, our great God, to restore this town and these people. In the name of Jesus Christ Your Son and our savior. Amen.

As you know, we are doing a very unusual thing this evening. We are combining prayers from the Christian tradition with that of ancient peoples, the Native Americans who lived on this very land before our ancestors arrived. Silver Crow Parker, Chief of the Comanche and a group of Americans of native heritage will conduct an ancient rain ceremony. We will begin the program with music. Myrtle Pevey will play the flute accompanied by Geraldine Whitfield on the violin with Clarajean White singing."

The crowd was spellbound as they listened like children at story time to beautiful harmony wafting across the valley, the notes seeming to disappear into the mountain. Tiny lights darted here and there like fireflies.

"Even if we don't get rain from all this, hearing *Amazing Grace* out here with our mountain is like having a peaceful cloud float over us." Lulu Belle leaned over to Odelia and Ed who were sitting beside her on blankets.

"It's inspirating, giving me chill bumps," Ed whispered and he smiled broadly. "And this is only the beginning."

The crowd applauded as Brother Hanson returned to the front of the audience and read a few Bible passages. Then the musical trio belted out *God Bless America*. The crowd stood and with spirits soaring, joined in singing at the tops of their voices.

Chief Silver Crow appeared, over a limestone crest at the edge of the mountain, backlighted by a fire. The crowd sighed at the sight of him in full native attire. His strong deep voice penetrated the air like a message straight from heaven. He introduced Bidai Choula of the Caddo, Charley Obe representing Alabama-Coushatta, and Elan Moore of the Apache. "We ask each of you to pray in your own way as we ascend to the top of the mountain to complete our part of the ceremony."

Native flutes played a haunting tune punctuated by distant drumbeats. The group turned and silently made their way up the side of the mountain, taking an almost invisible path, giving the illusion they were floating. Once they reached the summit they formed a line, raised their arms and began chanting, mesmerizing the crowd below. "He-ay-hee-ee. We call the Great Spirit." The top of the mountain erupted in colorful flames and smoke filled the air until the mountain disappeared. Then the sound of coyotes surrounded the area creating an unsettling, eerie atmosphere.

Reverend Hanson stepped to the front of the crowd. "Let us all leave the area in silence with praise and prayers in our hearts as the Lord and creator of the earth listens."

The sun's afterglow had disappeared and, except for the tiny lights, the area was pitch-black. Percy, more than ready to leave, wandered in circles searching for Etta Ruth and his partner.

"We're over here." Nick called out to Percy. "We have to talk."

"Oh, I see you now," said the mayor as he stumbled across the rocky field that served as the parking area. "Let's leave this God forsaken place."

"Come on to our house for a cup of coffee." Etta Ruth smiled.

"I'll follow you into town," said the tall man, not attempting a smile. *Damn, this has been one of the worse days of my life with Bea hating me and then me having to watch El Chico's stupid little show. I can't wait to see the last of the sparkle from Etta's flashy fake jewelry.*

Twenty minutes later he was sipping instant Maryland Club coffee in the Foremost's dining room. Graystone wondered how anyone could amass such a large collection of ruffles, velvet and ornamental knick-knacks, but then, this was Etta's house.

"I am glad we have this time for a visit. This is difficult for me to tell you, but," Graystone frowned as he paused to get their complete attention, "I've had a huge business opportunity present itself in Mexico. It's something I can't afford to turn down, so I am going to have to back out of our resort project."

"What! You can't do that!" Percy's face swelled up and turned as red as a pepper.

"Oh, no, Nick!" Etta Ruth got tears in her eyes and mascara began streaming down her face. "You can't leave me, us, like this!"

"I apologize to you both, but I'm sure you wouldn't want me to miss out on a huge deal. You have all the ideas, plans, and property options so you can do the project on your own."

"All we have is a bunch of debt." Percy was turning white and gasped for breath.

Graystone stood up and walked to the door. "I'll be in touch. I sincerely wish the two of you and El Chico lots and lots of luck and good fortune."

The couple didn't move or speak. All they could do was watch the familiar Lexus drive away. Etta Ruth tried to console her husband, but he was in a stupor like none she had ever seen before. "Honey pie, let's get you into bed. What you need is a good night's sleep. We can figure out what to do tomorrow."

All Percy could think of as he laid in bed was the nightmare he would have, the monsters that would attack from the mountain and Janelle's image beckoning him into an abyss. He closed his eyes and drifted off.

ENIGMA

The next morning Bea poured her coffee and strolled onto the porch to start her day. She wasn't surprised to see the same parched land that was there the day before and the day before that but she was surprised to see clouds still hanging around in the distance.

It was then she noticed the package. There was a large roll of papers, an envelope and a small box. Bea took the things inside and sat down at her dining table. She sipped her coffee and looked at the items before taking a deep breath and opening the envelope. A handwritten note and a check were inside.

Dearest Bea,

By the time you open this I will be gone, out of your life and the lives of all the good El Chico people forever. I know you won't believe me when I say I was going to tell you what happened and how it happened before you gave me the schematics, but now it doesn't matter anyway. Please know I am sorry and accept my sincere apology for all the wrong I have done. You are the dream woman of my life. Never did I think such a person existed; someone who is beautiful, smart and true. I wish you everything wonderful in the future and hope you will remember the times we shared with fondness."

Nick

P.S. The check enclosed is to reimburse the town of El Chico for funds they advanced to me."

Bea got tears in her eyes in spite of her anger at the man. *At least I know his feelings for me were sincere and I wasn't a total fool,* she thought as she sipped her coffee. After reading the note several times she opened the box. Inside was a gold bracelet with the Circle McP brand repeated in an intricate pattern around the entire piece. It was truly lovely and Bea knew, custom made for her.

Just as she began to unroll the mass of blueprints a loud rumbling sound in the distance startled her out of her reverie. The ground shook causing Bea's coffee cup to fall off the table. At first she thought she was imagining the movement. She hoped an underground gas line hadn't exploded. *What else could cause such a reaction?* She ran to the front porch and scanned the horizon for clues. Minutes later she saw Jake's pickup making its way across the field at top speed. She sprinted to the road to meet him.

"What in the hell was that?" she asked the cowboy.

"I don't have any idea but it was big, whatever it was. Hop in and let's get into town to see what happened." Jake drove down the highway as fast as the old truck allowed. When they reached Farnsworth's, it was evident the whole town heard and felt the jolt.

Doug was outside the café by the pumps looking at the mountain. "I think it came from the crest. I'm gonna go meet up with Ed and the firemen."

"Get in. We're going to see what we can find out."

Doug jumped into the truck bed and they joined the succession of vehicles jammed up to see what had happened. People across town were standing outside of homes and businesses, all looking upward.

Sheriff Darnell made his way through town, sirens going. "Please stay calm. Stay where you are and do not go to the mountain," he repeated over and over again on the car's speaker.

"I'll walk the rest of the way. It'll be faster." Doug jumped out of the truck bed and ran towards the high school.

"I think we're better off going back to the ranch and approaching the mountain from the backside." Jake turned the truck around and headed home.

When they got back to the ranch, Silver Crow was there with their horses saddled. "It's the mountain. Some kind of underground explosion."

"I'm not gonna ask how you know this." Jake mounted Pearce. "Bea, I guess there's no point tryin to get you to stay home."

"Nope. I'm goin with you two."

The three headed across the ranch, Buster and Sam following.

Meanwhile, Ed Hawkins and the volunteer firemen gathered around the fire truck he had driven to their regular meeting place at the school. "No emergencies in three years, then twice in one! This is why we practice, men."

The disheveled group boarded the old engine and Ed drove, siren blasting, to the base of the mountain, near where the ceremony had taken place the evening before.

"Do you think we're gonna blow up or have a volcano spewing red hot lava?" asked Chester.

"Oh my God, I hope not," Ed said, straightening his fireproof jacket.

"It knocked us down. I'm pretty sure the explosion came from the old mining area up top the rise." Buzzy and Annie Adams were standing outside the Ranger Motel and Sheriff Station. "I called Dalton as soon as the earth shook and boulders started rolling down the mountain. Cabin No. 1, the Jack Hays Suite, was nearly crushed."

The sheriff arrived, still blaring messages. His voice could be heard for blocks. "Attention emergency personnel: Gather 'round and we'll begin a military style search of the accident area."

Ed walked over to the car and leaned in the window. "We're all right here in front of you, Dalton. Cut the blasted speaker off. You're killin our eardrums."

With a frown, the man did as requested. It was unusual for him to get to use the loudspeaker and he liked the power of it. Once out of the car, he straightened his hat and gun belt. "Line up here, men, and I'll tell you the plan."

The sheriff led the way, pistol drawn and pointed ahead. Ed and the firemen followed up the side of the mountain. Lester Plunker took notes as he noticed various changes in the terrain.

"Look at that huge rock. It could've squashed the motel office." Buzzy was still shaking from the trauma.

"Lester, thanks for documenting what we find," said Dalton, trying to appear important. He returned the unused weapon to its holster.

The group screeched in unison when they felt another tremor.

"You think someone set off a load of dynamite?" Wilmur White's eyes were wide with fear.

"I don't think it's dynamite, but, remember Gavin, the engineer who talked with me less than a month ago? Well, he warned about the intra-geological makeup of the mountain. Ol Gav said our mountain has some explosive type elements deep underground."

"That could be it." The sheriff looked worried.

Ed motioned his group back to the truck. "I think we should leave the area and get some kind of expert to come look at this. Let's face it, sheriff, none of us knows what's happened."

"This might be the start of a big catastrophe. We need to talk with county emergency." The sheriff returned to his car to make the needed calls.

While Ed called Gavin, Buzzy Adams and the volunteers moved away from the base of the mountain and set up a roadblock to keep curious citizens away from the site.

☆ ☆ ☆

Crow led Jake and Bea to the east side of the mountain, arriving as the second tremor shook the ground. "I'd say there's something goin on and it's big." Jake frowned and looked at Bea. "I am not sure any of us should be here and it would mean a lot to me if you'd go back home."

"I'm sorry, Jake, but I'm goin wherever you're goin." Bea jerked

Starfire ahead.

"Let's go 'round to the old lake bed at the end of the mountain gap." Silver Crow turned, leading the group to what used to be El Chico's water source. Once there, the three dismounted to examine the terrain.

"Look at the size of these boulders, would ya?" Jake stood beside a rock that was as wide as he was tall. "This was some kind of explosion."

"Yeah. And feel that?" said Bea looking up. "Could it be raindrops?"

"Now you really have your imagination goin." Jake smiled his crooked smile.

"Don't be so damn smart. There **is** a small dark cloud overhead." The woman scowled.

"Look at this. It's just what I imagined." Silver Crow bent down and moved rocks with his hands. "It's water for sure. I think the explosion hit the underground spring and some moisture is coming up into the old lake."

"That would be a miracle!" Bea laughed out loud. "A miracle."

Jake, Bea, and Silver Crow sat down on scattered rocks as large as chairs and watched as water filled an area as big as a washtub, and grew to the size of a children's pool. The liquid moved like honey pouring from a jar.

"Yee-Ha! We have water!" Jake jumped up and down, picked Bea up and swung her around.

She joined Jake shocking the man with a big hug. "It's beginning to look like it did back in the old days when there was a real lake here. What a beautiful sight that would be."

Silver Crow was as excited as the two ranchers. "Let's get the horses and do some more lookin around. I wonder what else moved, and if any other springs are active." He ran to his horse. Bea and Jake followed.

Within an hour they found three more running springs on the Circle McP. Duke Five and the cows smelled the water and pawed at the ground where it was draining into their drinking pond.

"I'm hoping this means we don't ever have to have dudes visiting our ranch as payin guests." Jake grinned at Bea.

"That wasn't goin to happen anyway, Jake. But, I have to say you'd be a great campfire story teller if it did." Bea chuckled. "Nick fell for the legend just like we thought he would."

MIRACLES

By noon the entire town of El Chico knew the lake at the mountain was filling with precious water. At four o'clock the girls gathered at the Cut 'n Curl for a party scheduled to celebrate Juanita's recovery from cancer, now with a double purpose. The honoree was sitting in the center of a ring of plastic chairs surrounding a floral tablecloth-covered card table. Dips, chips, punch, and cookies were served. Streamers, twinkle lights, and flowers lined the countertops replacing the usual shampoos, sprays, brushes, and hair dryers.

"Let me toast Juanita Gutierrez! You never looked more gorgeous or more healthy. Your new short hairdo is adorable," said Lulu. "I guess my healin candle did the trick. That ol cancer went on its way, and maybe it helped bring water back to El Chico."

"I think we owe it all to Jesus. May we all thank God that He answered our prayers for complete recovery and for water," added Minnie Lee with a bowed head.

"My Auntie's tuna casserole added somethin to all the healin," stated Odelia with a huge smile as she twirled around the table.

One by one Bea stared at each lady in the room remembering how they used to gossip about Jaunita, glad they changed their attitudes. "Let's not forget Juanita's powerful vision, the one that looked like Silver Crow. The one who appeared mysteriously while she was on her deathbed, and today's miracle of the opened spring that occurred a few hours after the ceremony."

Juanita stood up and with a soft voice announced, "I don't guess we'll ever know how my healin happened but I do know I truly thank each of you here and all the many friends who helped Jose` and me through these hard months. The doctors say the chemotherapy worked, there's not a trace of the cancer anywhere in my body. It's a puzzlement, a real miracle. I have a special thanks to all of you who donated to the Juanita Gutierrez Fund Committee headed by Etta Ruth," added Juanita. "And where is that girl, anyway?"

"I am getting worried about her. I'd think she and the mayor would have been in the thick of the crowd talking about the explosion," Bea frowned. "Has anyone heard from them today?"

The group looked at each other and shook their heads.

"I tried to call her earlier but didn't get an answer." Minnie Lee looked worried. "Something is wrong. The mayor would have been leading the recovery efforts and it's not like Etta Ruth not to be here for an event she headed up."

"I'm going over to her house right now." Bea grabbed her purse and rushed out the door, drove the few blocks to the Foremost home and parked. She saw nothing unusual. The couple's cars were in the driveway. After ringing the doorbell, knocking on doors, and yelling, Etta Ruth finally answered.

"Etta Ruth, it's me, Bea." Bea was shocked at the woman's appearance. She looked like a ghost with black hair and seemed to be in a daze. "All the girls at the Cut 'n Curl were worried when you didn't show up for Juanita's party. You don't look well. Can I come it?"

Etta Ruth's eyes were swollen, her nose was running and she was shaking all over.

"Etta Ruth, honey, let's you sit down and you can tell me what's got you so upset."

Bea was surprised when Etta grabbed her and sobbed on her shoulder. Bea poured a glass of brandy, forcing Etta to drink a few sips. Still unable to speak, Etta pointed upstairs where she led Bea. There was Percy, in bed. Bea didn't have to look closely to know that he was as dead as dead could be.

☆ ☆ ☆

That evening Bea explained what she found at the Foremost home to Jake, Ed, Odelia, Doug, Wanda, Dolly, and Billy over dinner at On the Road Again.

The group was spellbound. "Once I got Etta calmed down we called the sheriff and he made all the arrangements to get county coroner and law enforcement to the scene. Doc Wilson came fast but had to call his friend over at the county seat to help. Once that doctor got there he gave Etta a shot. Minnie Lee came and took care of her. She'll stay as long as she's needed."

"I guess Doc Wilson didn't think a vet could fix Etta's problem. We're gonna have to get a human doctor in El Chico," Dolly added.

Ed continued the story. "Dalton told me Percy died in his sleep from an apparent heart attack. Poor Etta Ruth was awakened in the night with him screaming from a nightmare but she said he did that almost every night. They went back to sleep and in the morning she got up to make their coffee while he stayed asleep, or she thought he was asleep. When she called him to come join her in the kitchen, he didn't come and when she tried to wake him up she realized he was dead."

Bea added, "I think what upset her the most, was that she was right beside him when he died and she didn't even know it, couldn't do a thing to help the poor man. When the earth shook, Etta was scared out of her wits. That's probably what sent her into full shock." Bea nodded her head. "It was really a sad scene.

A week later the mayor's funeral was over. Etta Ruth was still at home recovering from the shock of widowhood. The Cut 'n Curl ladies brought food and took turns staying with her.

The rest of the town was celebrating the *El Chico Times Gazette*'s report on the findings of Lone Star Engineering. The firm, headed by Ed Hawkins's friend, said they were certain the main spring leading from the aquifer was as open as it had been many centuries ago. The underground implosion was caused by deep-earth pressure. Various elements, including gypsum, silica, and angelite were heated as if they were in a super pressure cooker. Eventually a fissure, like a giant underground pipe, drove water to the earth's surface. El Chico would have a water supply for many years. The report also explained that while this was a good thing, the aquifer would depend on rainwater to replenish it. The wells alone wouldn't supply enough water for agriculture and grazing land.

In another front-page story the city council announced the pump leading to the water tower would be installed with city funds that had been returned by H_2O Engineering from the cancelled pipeline project and their pipes would flow, not drip. El Chico would have water. However, they were reminded, there was still a drought crisis, that they must conserve water, and the ranchers must have continuing rain to exist.

WEE SMALL HOURS

Jake hadn't slept well for months. This was unusual for him. He stared at the ceiling in his small cabin. A full moon reflected off the Cottonwood tree outside his window casting eerie shadows.

For most of his adult life Jake lived alone in the near-wilderness of the Circle McP Ranch. Until recently he never felt lonely. The solitude of the cowboy life suited him. After Sue died, over twenty years ago, he didn't want anyone too close. Just when he was beginning to like having a constant companion, she had been killed. If he was honest with himself, he knew adjusting to married life had been a struggle, even back then.

As he stared at the moving ghostlike shapes dancing around the room, his mind retraced life when it included Sue. The first time he saw her was at the county rodeo grounds where he was scouting the bulls, one of which he'd ride that night. She was leaning against a fence railing, long brown hair blowing across her face. All he could see was her mouth and its full lips. She was laughing as she brushed her thick mane away, revealing the most beautiful brown eyes he'd ever seen. Two of his cowboy friends, the Rowland brothers, were talking to her so he walked straight across the rodeo arena, jumped the fence and joined the group.

"Hi there. I'm Jake Johnson, buddy of these two mavericks. He reached out his hand to shake hers. She laughed, put her hand in his and smiled.

Curt slapped Jake on the back. "Sue, before I introduce you to this here scoundrel I want to warn you. He's known far and wide as a lady's man so be on guard."

"Don't pay no attention to these fellas. You know how brothers can only take up for each other. They just want to keep all the pretty ladies to themselves." Jake laughed. "Besides these ugly boys are married and have a dozen children between them."

"Jake you are a liar, doin' all you can to convince Miss Susan Avery you're worth her time. You should know she's a star barrel racer, runner-up state champ last year. Sue, beware of Jake. He is a badass bull rider just waitin to get thrown."

"Gentlemen, I am flattered by all this attention, but I've got some rodeo things to do before this evening's event. I'm sure I'll see you around." Jake and his friends watched as the woman walked away, swaying her hips in a way only western girls in boots can do. She turned around, looked at Jake, winked and waved with a big smile on her face.

"Oh Lord! I've been had. Ain't she the prettiest thing you've ever laid your eyes on; and spunky, too." Jake looked at the brothers who were laughing out loud.

"I've never seen you get taken like this before, Jake. Watch out or you'll be roped and tied in record time."

"Yeah. And maybe I won't even care!" said Jake.

Six months later he married Sue and they moved to a mobile home on the ranch where he worked.

A coyote howled in the distance and a stiff breeze scraped the tree's branches across Jake's roof. Sam raised his head and looked at his master and then rested his head on his haunches again. This time he didn't close his eyes knowing Jake wouldn't be in bed long.

Jake remembered how Sue would turn and wink and wave each time she left him and that's how he preferred to remember her, not as a broken body covered by the heap of twisted metal and wood the tornado left behind. He shook his head praying for some sleep but it wouldn't come. At times like these there was nothing to do but get up and ride.

Jake was on Pearce's back ten minutes later, slowly cantering across the barren plains of the Circle McP with Sam close behind.

The recent earthshaking and opened springs had helped the parched land. The mesquite were green, but the grass was sparse and the arroyos mostly empty. Pearce made his way up the embankment of the mountain, knowing the trail well from past visits, he climbed to the top where his owner could see for miles.

Jake dismounted and went to the limestone outbreak. He made his way to the flat surface where he sat and gazed and thought. The two years after Sue died were a blur of part time jobs, stacks of empty liquor bottles and cheap motel rooms. When he was hired for the Circle Mc P's spring round up he began to feel like himself again. Henry and Mary McPherson were long time rodeo friends and knew about his loss. They insisted he eat family dinner with them each night. Harold was home from college helping with the round up and Bea, then fourteen, participated. Soon he was laughing and sharing a life with the McPhersons, feeling like a family member. Even then he knew Bea had a teen-aged crush on him, so he made it clear he was an old man, a peer of her dad's, although he was only twenty-four.

For the past twelve years, it had been just the two of them, Jake and Bea, running the Circle McP. Bea living alone in the big ranch house and Jake living in the small cabin on the backside of the acreage. Jake smiled thinking of Bea and how brave she was after her parents died; how she had become a first rate rancher. He realized she had the same kind of spunk that Sue had. Maybe that's why he'd always been attracted to her and made himself keep a certain aloof manner when around her; that was until lately.

As Jake gazed across the grasslands he thought of Bea; her thick, curly, red hair and turquoise eyes, the freckles across her nose, the way she frowned when she wasn't getting her way and the smile when she did. He couldn't mark the time, the exact incident when he fell in love with her, but there was a time when he realized he wanted to be with her, to hold her, to make love to her. Somehow he'd managed to navigate the days, months and years with her, putting his feelings aside, being her business partner, foreman and friend, never stepping over the line to where he'd really like to be. He was too old, too set in his ways and she, well, Bea could have any man she set her mind to.

Jake took off his hat and slammed it into the ground. "Damn it to hell. Why had that Nicholas Graystone interfered? Bea and I were perfect friends. No pressure, just here for each other. That big bastard from Dallas!"

Jake stood and looked across the ranch. "I hope the man is rotting in hell. To think he almost had Bea." Jake jumped down from the ledge and stalked around, stomping his feet. "Maybe I should feel grateful to that rat for making me see how I cain't lose her."

As daylight appeared over the horizon Jake thought about what Silver Crow said to him and it began to make good sense. Jake rubbed Sam behind the ears. "Hey boy. What if Crow is right and Bea does have some romantic feelings for me? The sunrises are gettin fewer and fewer for us and this ole earth is spinning faster and faster. Crow accuses me of being a fool and I'm thinkin he's right."

Jake whistled to Pearce, remounted, and the trio made their way down the mountain and across the ranchland following the first of the sun's rays. He saw Bea's house in the distance, the long porch highlighted as if in a movie set. Jake squinted. What in the hell? There was Bea, sitting on the porch as if waiting for something. Jake picked up his pace hoping nothing was wrong.

She stood up, shaded her eyes with her hand and walked to meet Jake, Pearce and Sam. "My God, Jake. What in the world are you doing out this early? It's not even six yet."

Jake jumped off his horse and walked straight to her. "Bea, are you okay?"

"I'm totally fine. Just haven't been able to sleep lately."

"Me neither." He took a deep breath, looked at the ground and then at Bea. "Before I lose my nerve I've got to talk to you."

Bea stared up at him with wide eyes, expecting bad news.

"Bea, I love you. Probably 've been in love with you for years, but just didn't think it was right to think of you the way I did plus I didn't want to spoil our friendship. I know I'm mostly a confirmed loner but I've come to know that I live for the times we're together. I know my life ain't worth a flip without you and want to wake up the in the morning and go to bed at night with you beside me. I cain't sleep or eat anymore without you. I think I'm a little crazy over this, and I cain't go another day without you knowing how I feel."

Tears streamed down Bea's face. She was afraid she was going to faint.

"On no, Bea. I didn't mean to make you cry." Jake reached out and Bea stepped into his arms.

She felt the warmth of his body encircle her. "You stupid, stupid cowboy. I could kill you. I waited and waited and was just about to give up on you. You knew I loved you when I was fourteen, and I've never stopped. Damn it, Jake, we wasted so much time."

He put his hand under her chin, raised her head and gazed into her eyes. Then he kissed her long and hard with all the passion he'd held inside for so long. She took him by the hand, opened the front door, and led him to her bedroom, welcoming him all the way into her life.

BLUEPRINT

"Ed, we want you to run for the open Mayor's position. We'll back you a hundred percent." Bea poured drinks for the group assembled around her dining table.

"There's no one more qualified. You know El Chico better than anyone. I wondered why you didn't run before." Jake clinked glasses with Ed and they took swigs of the Jack Daniels.

"Odelia and I've discussed this and we're ready to be completely committified to the election and position if I'm the winner.

Odelia reached over and patted Ed's hand in support. "Ed and I think Bea should run on the slate with him. It's time El Chico had a woman's voice officially on the council and, Bea, you are the perfect candidate."

The small group stood and cheered. "Ed and Bea! Ed and Bea!"

"We will have some opponents who are supporting Wilmur, and the council will have some legal issues to address having to do with Percy's and Etta Ruth's involvement in the bogus pipeline project," Bea said.

Ed spoke as if he'd already been elected. "The way I see this, is we should drop the entire thing. Graystone returned the town's funds and disappeared from the face of the earth. Because Etta is in default on all the real estate holdings, she stands a chance of losing everything, even her home. I don't want to punish a widow."

Bea stood up, walked across the room and returned with a large rolled-up blueprint. "Maybe you should see this. Nick left it on the porch when he took off."

Jake helped unroll the documents. "This here's a plan that might just change the city's future. As much as I couldn't stand Graystone, he did have good business insight, except for the damned dude ranch idea."

"By God. This is a plan that utilizes all the properties in default over on the east side." Ed pointed here and there at locations on the schematic. "This is downright amazing. How in the world can we make this project happen?"

For the next two hours Ed, Odelia, Doug, Wanda, Bea and Jake discussed the possibilities of building the resort that was once the secret plan Graystone proposed to the Foremosts.

A few weeks later, in private, Bea went to a drawer in her bureau and removed the gold bracelet, knowing she would never wear it. She rotated it, admiring its beauty, thinking of the unusual man who gave it to her.

No one but Bea knew she received a congratulatory note from Nicholas Graystone. Enclosed in the envelope were copies of the Gazette's articles about the upcoming election's slate of candidates and plans for an El Chico resort. There was no return address but it was mailed with postage stamps from Bolivia.

ON THE ROAD AGAIN

A nasty dust storm skirted El Chico, forcing strong wind gusts through the town. Haze diffused the horizon, leaving little demarcation between land and sky. Old papers and leaves twisted across vacant lots and down streets. Long dead tree branches bent double and broke off dangling like giant ghost-house chandeliers. A coat of gritty dirt covered cars, tractors and roofs.

Dolly and an oversized pan of potato salad were almost crushed by the back door from the force of the squall when she tried to enter On the Road Again.

"Put it over by the brisket," said Billy. Tying a red bandana over his long gray braids he added, "El Chico deserves a little barbecue and celebratin."

"I know it, honey. We're lucky there was a cow left alive to butcher for the brisket.

Hugging his wife from behind and grabbing her ample breasts he said, "Hey baby, wanna take a break from all this cookin and do a little cookin of our own?"

"Get outta here, you sex-crazed man," Dolly giggled as she tasted their special barbecue sauce.

She hummed when she checked the streamers hanging across the dining area. She then yelled at Billy as she once again wrestled the heavy back door, and scurried across the street to their small frame house. "Oh my God! They'll be here in less than an hour! I hardly have time to change into my party outfit."

Back in the late 1800s, the restaurant's building had been the El Chico Opera House. The structure was three stories tall with a vaulted ceiling. Remnants of gold leafed carvings still encircled the open room and the huge double front doors. In the beginning, the building was host to prestigious traveling troops presenting performances like *H.M.S. Pinafore* and *The Bohemian Girl*. As the years went by and the town's economic boom went bust, the elaborate theater became a hardware store and then a dry goods emporium.

It stood vacant and decaying for years until Billy and Dolly made a deal with the bank and turned it into the present barbecue haven. On the Road Again gave them a purpose and a home. The old opera house stage was long gone, but the balcony served as a fine substitute. Just inside the ornate front doors an arched alcove functioned as a parking lot for Billy's and Dolly's Harleys, where they could be viewed from the sidewalk.

Billy knew how to smoke a brisket until it was tender and tasty. Dolly served, and did the business arithmetic. Billy had tired of traveling with Willie and his band, but liked the excitement of show business. He reasoned he and his wife could gather an audience because of the food and the opportunity to hear live music. He could tolerate the grind of managing a restaurant if he could continue performing.

While Dolly forced her body into skin-tight jeans and a low-necked blouse, put on her black and silver boots and bright red Stetson, Billy set up the bar. Because El Chico was dry, he lined up the liquor and glasses on a table in the men's room and cooled the beer in an old galvanized watering tub in the kitchen closet. He knew Sheriff Dalton wouldn't mind because he'd be enjoying the evening like everyone else in town.

Dolly made her way back to the café holding tight to her hat afraid her bleach-blond hairpieces would blow all the way to Lubbock.

Bea, red curls standing out in all directions from the harsh winds, arrived and began helping Billy arrange the Texas-themed paper plates, napkins, and tablecloths on the shuffleboard commandeered as the food buffet.

"Jake dropped me off, but had to go back to the ranch to check up on the livestock. The wind is fierce; blew us all over the road. There's such a sandstorm going he was sure it would panic Duke Five. He'll be back as soon as he can."

The Methodists and Baptists had services early in the day giving parishioners time to go home and change from church to party clothes. Everyone attending would contribute to the dinner or pay five dollars.

Odelia was bringing Ed's favorite chocolate chip cookies (the recipe reputed to be Neiman Marcus's very own, bought for a thousand dollars by a fellow Texan). Wilma and Doug would bring her pies and Minnie Lee promised her queso dip with jalapenos.

Once the table was set and brisket ready, Billy, Dolly, and Bea listened to the jukebox and sang. Billy warmed up his guitar. Then the trio just sat and stared at the decorations, waiting and worrying. "Where are the people? It's way past time for them to start gettin here." Billy paced and Bea solo-danced around the sawdust floor.

"Maybe we should just eat a brisket sandwich," said a teary-eyed Dolly. "I don't think no one is comin."

As she completed her sentence the enormous front doors blew open, forced by the blustery wind. Silver Crow Parker appeared, framed by the lavish molding, black braids blowing around his dark, chiseled face, the wind shrieking in the background. He was dressed in black, except for the bright red duster billowing like wings behind his muscular body. His piercing blue eyes scanned the empty room and he spoke in his clear baritone voice.

"Dolly and Bea, call everyone you can reach and tell them to get ready because Jake and I are picking them up. The air is as thick as molasses and feels like sandpaper. It's making folks afraid to leave their houses. We can't let this nasty storm ruin our celebration. Billy, keep the brisket hot and the beer cold. We'll be back." He left as quickly as he appeared.

Over the next hour Silver Crow and Jake went house to house in Bea's Escalade picking up as many people as they could stuff into the vehicle, delivering them, a group at a time, to the restaurant.

Once the bulk of the crowd made their way through the howling sandstorm, Billy's band was going strong.

A banner with "The Swinging Singing Rangers" printed in bold letters was displayed on the wall behind the band. The lively group was perched on the balcony surrounded by hundreds of colorful lights pulled from Bea's Christmas decoration box. The eager performers overlooked the main part of the restaurant, now a dance floor. Because Billy had no way to hoist the piano up to the loft, Mable Pevey pounded the ivories from the hallway outside the men's room, dodging partygoers anxious for Jack Daniels or Lonestar refills.

Lulu Belle leaned over and spoke in Wilma's ear, "Look at the Plunkers. Marjorie is wearing her blue party dress, the one she's worn to every social for the past ten years and that Lester, he's so stiff he looks like his underwear is starched.

"Look closer, Lulu. You can see them tappin their feet. Cain't help themselves but enjoy the music."

Herb and Mary Nelle Matson, the best two steppers in the county, took the floor gliding and turning, Violet Cartwright and Odelia Hawkins danced with each other since their spouses were part of the "Rangers." Once Dolly and Bea got the food arranged on the buffet table they joined the group spinning around the floor to *Waltz Around Texas.*

Then, Jake cut in, whirling Bea in a circle. Their eyes locked and he smiled as he reached down and kissed her lightly on the lips. Bea squeezed his hand, laughed out loud and whirled into another circle. She kissed him back.

"Just look at that. Jake and Bea dancin like a real couple and kissin." Ed leaned over to Billy as they strummed.

By nine o'clock stomachs were full and feet were sore. Suddenly, Billy grabbed the mic, "Listen up everyone. I said BE QUIET! LISTEN!"

The partiers became as still as a photograph. The sound of roaring wind was gone, replaced with silence and then with the pitter-patter of rain hitting the metal roof. Dolly ran to the front of the building and swung the doors wide open, framing the West Texas sky. Small, then large raindrops fell on the dirty highway creating little puffs of dust. At first the crowd stared, fixated, as if seeing a mirage.

"Rain. It's real wet rain fallin into El Chico. Perseparation!" Ed jumped up and down and danced like he was a kid. Then someone else yelled and others joined in, clapping and screaming with delight. Uninhibited, they ran outdoors looking upward, arms outspread to allow the cool wetness to wash faces, and soak hair. Their clothes were damp but spirits as sunny as the skies they'd endured for years.

Rain fell in earnest. Not a storm, but a steady shower filled the countryside. Tiny puddles turned into mini-streams filtering down dormant gullies and into the landscape. People throughout El Chico stood in their yards, sat on porches or walked through puddles, boots caked with mud, letting their souls absorb the rain.

As faint as a breath, Mable Pevey began playing the piano and Billy joined in on the harmonica. Clarajean's pure, rich voice resonated across the town of El Chico.

"Amazing Grace.
How sweet the sound.
That saved a wretch like me!
I once was lost but now am found;
Was blind, but now I see.

When we've been there ten thousand years,
Bright shining as the sun,
We've no less days to sing God's praise
Than when we first begun."

* *Amazing Grace* was written by John Newton (1725-1807)

ACKNOWLEDGEMENTS

The story of El Chico would never have happened had I not spent my childhood surrounded by my mother, her seven brothers, two sisters, their spouses and a bunch of cousins. All grew up in the trans Pecos area of Texas. Vacations, family reunions and funerals were held in their hometown. The gatherings were wild and happy occasions (even the funerals).

While the characters in my book are fictitious they combine parts and sometimes the whole of these colorful Texans. Each had big personalities and their own special senses of humor that included laughing hardest at themselves. Their exceptional work ethic and entrepreneurial spirits directed their careers. They taught me to always look for the good and positive in mankind and the world and best of all, they were full of love, big physical-affectionate hug-filled love.

I apologize for any flaws or deficiencies in telling about the very real drought in Texas. As I write, the land is drying up taking its nourishment with it. Telling about the event that brings water and how the town of El Chico has the good fortune to have a geological miracle occur is fictitious. I only hope a miracle does occur and the grass lands return as they were when sixty million Buffalo roamed and Native Americans had the freedom to live and travel with them.

After writing several short stories about El Chico, my writing partners in Sonoma wanted more. This provided the momentum to create a novel about the town and characters that became our imaginary friends. This is their project as well as mine. Thanks to Sonoma Writing Alliance members: Steve Bakalyar, Maureen Bruce, Fran Dayan, Klarise Davis, John Field, Lucille Hamilton, Michael James, Dave Lewis, Robyn Makaruk, Michael Miley, Helen Rowntree, Joan Shepherd, Janet

Wentworth, and Jean Wong. Special thanks goes to Klarise Davis, Jean Wong and Kira Calanzaro who went above and beyond to help me through the editing and publishing process. More thanks to other Sonoma writers who inspire and motivate me: Michelle Wing, Judy Lerner, Ed and Gaynell Reyno, Sandra Witmer, Donna McLaughlin, Caryl Englehorn, LA King and Donna Campbell. Thanks to my dear friend, a true Texan, Nancy Corkill for encouragement and support.

My brother, David Strauss, knew about El Chico from the beginning. He understood in his bones about this imaginary place because he'd spent his childhood as my sidekick and adulthood as my best friend. He knows the people that stimulated me to write. His memories helped ignite mine and his knowledge of Texas history was invaluable.

My friend, Mark Flowers, listened week after week, often to the same tales revised over and over again. I could gauge the quality of the words by his expressions and truthful comments. If a native San Franciscan liked a story set in Texas, it couldn't be all bad. His patience and encouragement kept me writing.

I thank my children and grandchildren for their reassurance, inspiration and praise as I muddled through life and began exercising my late-in-life passion to write. Elizabeth Grivas; Christine, Jon and Emma Curry; Bart, Erica, Colton, Ozro and Manda Dillashaw, you are the loves of my life.

Without my editor, Deb Carlen, this novel would be stuffed in a drawer, never published. Her keen eye and experience guided me throughout the process of developing tales of a small Texas town and its people into a story.

Patty Coleman is the force that put the manuscript into a design and format suitable for print. It's an actual book because of her ability to ready the words stored in my computer ... all in the correct order, for the publisher.

A very special thanks, to Andy Weinberger, owner of Reader's Books in Sonoma, who invigorates, supports and inspires writers, especially the Sonoma variety. Reader's Books' Random Acts, managed by Catherine Sevenau and Chris Giovachinni, gives local writers a venue to read their work to an audience each month. The applause spurs us onward. Accolades to Marlene Cullen whose Write Spot and Petaluma Writers Forum helps to educate and motivate Sonoma's writers.

I would never have attempted to put any creative words on paper had not John Curry and Janice Crow Curry invited me to attend a workshop at their Starwae Inn in 2007. Adair Lara inspired and taught me to begin to write. "Write everyday, and keep at it even if you only copy the back of a cereal box." As she already knew, if a person wants to write and puts words on paper daily, they'll be on their way.

I've learned a piece of work is never finished. Each time I look at a paragraph I see something to revise, to improve. But I've also learned if a person wants to share their work they have to let it go with its imperfections. So, this is my story of the town and people of El Chico. I hope you enjoy getting to know them as much as I have.

Meta Strauss transplanted to Sonoma, California in 2005 thinking she left Texas behind forever. But the bigger-than-life state is not so easy to abandon and *Saving El Chico* persisted in taking shape as she wrote fiction and memoir in her new, enlightened life in California.

Made in the USA
San Bernardino, CA
27 February 2016